D0860059

Dust to Dust

Also by Timothy Findley

NOVELS
The Piano Man's Daughter
Headhunter
The Last of the Crazy People
The Butterfly Plague
The Wars
Famous Last Words
Not Wanted on the Voyage
The Telling of Lies

NOVELLA
You Went Away

SHORT FICTION
Dinner Along the Amazon
Stones

PLAYS
Can You See Me Yet?
John A.—Himself
The Stillborn Lover

NON-FICTION
Inside Memory: Pages From a Writer's Workbook

Timothy Findley

Dust to Dust

Stories

HarperCollins*PublishersLtd*

Several of these stories have been published prior to this collection, or will be published simultaneously: "Abracadaver" in *Prairie Fire*, Winter 1997, Vol. 17 #4; "Kellerman's Windows" in *Blood & Aphorisms*, Winter 1997, No. 25; "Americana" in *Quarry*, 1991, Vol. 40 #1; "A Bag of Bones" in *Exile*, Winter 1997, No. 21; and "The Madonna of the Cherry Trees" in *Descant*, Winter 1996, Vol. 27 #4.

http://www.harpercollins.com/canada

First edition

Canadian Cataloguing in Publication Data

Findley, Timothy, 1930–
Dust to dust

ISBN 0-00-224409-8

I. Title.

PS8511.I38D87 1997   C813'.54   C96-931915-0
PR9199.3.F56D87 1997

97 98 99 ❖ HC 10 9 8 7 6 5 4 3 2 1

Printed and bound in the United States

We humans, dead and alive, are not and never have been alone. Some of this dust is dog-dust, horse-dust and cat-dust—the dust of beloved animals. For those who have shared my life, my thanks.

Dust to Dust

Dust • 3

Kellerman's Windows • 35

Abracadaver • 47

A Bag of Bones • 83

Come as You Are • 117

Hilton Agonistes • 151

Americana • 165

Infidelity • 175

The Madonna of the Cherry Trees • 193

Dust

You might as well just be dust. Sweep up dust and it might contain a fragment of Caesar or Cleopatra, anybody, one day it might be me, but that is not immortality, that is just dust.

—Francis Bacon
Interviewed by William Burroughs
Guardian Weekly, May 17, 1992

THE HOTEL ATHENE, on the island of Paros, is within a twenty-minute walk from the town of Naoussa. Guests very often give themselves the pleasure of strolling, early in the evening, along the dusty road to one of the small cafés whose chairs all face the sea. There, with wine or ouzo, the guests will sit and watch the fishing boats returning with the day's catch.

Oliver Sher had never been to Greece before. But his friend had just died and they had intended to make this journey together from London to the Aegean. Now, he was making it alone, but for them both.

His friend—as some would say, his *companion*—had not been expected to die so soon. But there were sudden complications and the cancer took a turn for the worse: in two short weeks, he was gone. Not dead—but gone. Oliver Sher had still not mentioned the D-word. Even in his mind, he excised it by singing in a loud voice, no matter what he was doing, no matter where he was. The voice—that might have shattered eardrums if anyone else had been able to hear it—was entirely inside his head. This was where Oliver Sher did most of his living and nearly all of his talking and certainly all of his singing. He was not deaf, but his friend had been. René. Oliver's most expressive speech was spoken with his hands.

His café of choice on the waterfront was The Dionysus, where the chairs were painted yellow and the tables painted blue. A family of red-haired cats would come out and sit at his feet and he would slip them bits of fish or seafood saved especially from lunch. He ate very little himself. René, by the end of his life, had been paper-thin—and Oliver had wasted with him. Now, perhaps, he would start to eat again—but not just yet. A certain tribute—paid while staring at his emaciated self in the mirror—must still be made to the memory of René's body. And his suffering.

The one thing Oliver would not—could not—give up, in spite of the fact that René had died of lung cancer, was cigarettes. And so, the fingers of one hand dipped eternally towards the ashtray while the fingers of the other fed the cats. His drink was rosé wine. Others, watching him, declared that he was *a character*—but this was not so. He was not the least bit eccentric, merely self-defined.

One brilliant evening of early stars and a crescent moon, Oliver Sher was seated in his place at The Dionysus when an incident occurred that was to prove catastrophic in nature, though not until some days later. What actually happened seemed of little importance—a child went running amongst them chasing a cat and calling out: *chat enragé! Chat enragé!*

Oliver's knowledge of French was mostly in his fingers, since his communications with René, in his companion's native language, had usually entailed a lot of signing. Clearly, however, the child— a boy of five or six—was convinced the cat had tried to harm him and was seeking some kind of revenge. As fate would have it, Oliver later decided, the cat and the child made straight for his table. Cats, he loved—but children, he hated.

Oliver's five red cats went flying in all directions as the boy fell down—the fall deliberate—and seized the fleeing feline with both hands. Oliver stood up. His wine had been spilled into his lap.

The boy had not been hurt in the least, but the cat he held was in trouble. As the child rose back into view from beneath the table, his hands were around the animal's neck and it was scream-ing—or attempting to.

Oliver stared, his mouth beginning to open. How do you say: *what is happening?* in French? His fingers moved before he spoke.

"*Qu'est-ce qui se passe?*"

No sooner had he spoken than the boy looked up at him with a smile that Oliver would never forget. The child's expression was demonic. He was killing the cat.

Oliver leaned across the table and seized the boy by the collar of his shirt. Though he spoke in French, his panic was in English.

"Let go!" And then: "LET GO!"

The child stared. Oliver shook him.

The cat—still alive, though barely—fell to the stones.

Oliver did not let go of the child. In fact he took him by the arm and held him even tighter. The boy's expression had been electrifying—so clearly the expression of someone with a monstrous appetite for inflicting pain that Oliver could not bear to set him loose for fear of what the child might do.

It was then—to everyone's relief—that a man came hurrying forward, calling: "*Monsieur! Monsieur! Assez! Assez! S'il vous plaît!* "

Oliver let go.

The child said nothing.

The father—it must have been the father—took the boy's hand, but did not address him. Instead, he looked at Oliver Sher with an expression that needed no voice. *Don't*, it said, *tell anyone what you have seen my son doing.* Then it said: *please.*

Oliver nodded.

The man said: "*merci, monsieur* "—almost inaudibly—and turning his child aside, walked away with him, hand in hand.

Oliver sat down.

The waiter came.

Oliver held out his emptied carafe and said: *more*—a desire that is understood in any language.

The hotel itself played a role in what follows. Like Oliver, it sat there and watched.

Everyone agreed it was an architectural wonder, rising from the landscape as if the landscape itself had given birth to it. Oliver liked to imagine the moment when the architect first encountered the scene. Standing on the heights, he would have seen the stony flats descending to the water's edge and all their ancient flights of tumbled walls, pulled down by time. It was a dream location.

Out in the bay there was an island occupied by a single white mosque. Its walls were stippled with laurel leaves and shadows cast by olive trees. Its shuttered windows were blind and its doors were never opened. No one could tell you why it stood alone or why it was that no one ever went to worship there. Even people sunning themselves offshore on yachts looked at it only through binoculars. Whose island was it—and whose white walls? *The gods'*, somebody said. And might have been right. The mosque, after all, stood in Greece, where Nature was the first religion.

Looking down from his hotel balcony, Oliver Sher was entranced by the view. Far out beyond the bay and its embrace, the ancient sea was the colour of René's eyes—blue with flecks of green and the mauve that is seen in the depths of violets. Along the shore, above a rise of land, the roofs and walls of Naoussa shimmered, barely more than a mirage. On the terrace beyond the pool, a young man—shirtless—was sweeping a cloud of dust to the farthest edge, where it floated for a moment like a magic carpet above the stones. Immediately below Oliver's balcony, the latticework of a grass awning was spread above a group of white tables and chairs and, beyond that, a smattering of white umbrellas sheltering silent couples who were eating breakfast.

Oliver waited, having looked at his watch. Before descending to drink his orange juice and coffee, he wanted to see if an event he had witnessed on his first morning would be repeated. To date, for one whole week, a small rubber ball—of a size that would fit in the palm of your hand—had bounced, as if with a life of its own, across the stones of the terrace and into the pool. The ball was yellow—the colour of a daffodil—and it appeared every morning precisely at 8:15.

Now, it was 8:14.

Down on the terrace, beside the silent couples, a lonely, would-be swimmer was poised at the edge of the water. He was of medium height and slight of build, though not—like Oliver—thin. He might have been thirty years old. Thirty-five. He was wearing the sort of bathing suit that declared at once that his usual swimming place was the sea. It was not a European *slip*, but a North American—probably Californian—surfer's suit that reached his knees.

"Oh, do get away from the pool before the ball arrives," Oliver muttered out loud. He was used to talking to himself. Since René could never hear him—so long as Oliver turned his back—he could say anything he liked. He could say: *you bugger!* And he had. He could say: *fuck off!* And he had. He could even say: *I hate your fucking deafness—and your fucking disease—and your fucking demands! Piss off!* And he had. But only once. Only once, when it had all gone on too long, and Oliver was at his wits' end.

There, now. 8:15—and the would-be swimmer still poised.

Oliver held his breath.

Please.

Yes. There it was.

The ball came bouncing across the stones: once—twice—three times. *Splash.*

The would-be swimmer stared at it.

The ball had been braver than he was. There it was in the water. This was Oliver's thought—not the would-be swimmer's.

The would-be swimmer took it as a cue, however, and jumped in, feet first.

"Now, everything is ruined," Oliver said out loud.

Still, he waited, wanting to see what the consequence would be.

The usual figure appeared—the one that on every other morning had followed the bouncing ball to the terrace and retrieved it from the pool. This was a man of barely human height—or so it seemed to Oliver, who was six-foot-two. He was five feet tall at the most and wore, inevitably, a yellow bathing cap and a pair of black rugby shorts. He was barrel-chested and bandy-legged and maybe sixty or sixty-five years old. He never spoke to anyone; his nationality was entirely a mystery. He also seemed not to speak because something was wrong. Oliver surmised that perhaps the man had suffered a stroke. He moved like that—the way the victims of a stroke had moved in the Royal Victoria, whenever Oliver had passed them in the hall on his way to René's cancer ward. *They are not stroke victims—they are stroke survivors*, Oliver repeated dutifully. *Yes, doctor.*

Now, the little man came forward and stared at the would-be swimmer swimming towards his ball.

Don't! Oliver shouted—silent.

But the would-be swimmer—who swam rather well, if the truth be told—reached out and took the ball in his hand.

Oliver heard him say: "yours?" And watched as the ball was thrown back onto the terrace beyond the stroke survivor's reach.

"You bloody fool," said Oliver. "Now, he won't be able to pick it up."

Still, he would try. Giving the would-be swimmer a reproach-ful—almost a mournful—look, the stroke survivor turned away. Would-be hung at the side of the pool, his legs dangling down, foreshortened by the water, and he watched as the yellow bathing cap, which matched the ball, went amongst the tables, chairs and elaborate pots of geraniums, looking for its lost companion.

It *is* his *companion,* Oliver thought. He can barely live without that ball. It's his therapeutic lover. They must have given it to him when he was released from hospital. He could use it to regain lost capabilities—co-ordination—an obedient body, able to respond to his orders. *Fetch!* And *carry! Squeeze!* The daily lexicon of commands that everybody who has not endured a stroke takes absolutely for granted. *Shave! Bathe! Brush your teeth!*

Imagine not being able to brush your teeth ...

Oliver could no longer bear to watch. He would descend and, if he must, help in the search for the ball. Thinking this, he turned away and went back into his room. Before departing for the lower regions, however, he paused to brush his teeth. Not because he needed to—but because he could.

Preferring the pinstripe shadows of the grass lattice, Oliver chose a table in its shade and placed a pillow in the chair. He was now so thin that the bones supporting his buttocks needed padding. Speaking in English, he ordered *one of those*—caffe latte—and *two of those*—a double serving of blood-orange juice. He would take no solid food until noon. At lunch, perhaps he would have a plate of lettuce and tomatoes—something acid, to push away his hunger. Plus smoked salmon—imported—served with lemon and capers. Ignoring the salmon, he would suck the lemon and eat the capers on thick white pieces of bread whose pores would drink in the juices left from the rest of his meal. In his room, he kept a box of zip-lock bags into one of which he would place the fish, and set the bag in a bath of cold water run into the bathroom sink. It would stay there until his evening walk into town. Five red cats and perhaps the one he had saved from the boy would dine that night on salmon.

Now, with the morning's first cigarette in hand, Oliver watched the other guests foregather for the day's beginning. The problem of the yellow ball had been solved by the time he had descended in the lift. The stroke survivor was seated to his left, covered now with a thick, black terrycloth robe, and the ball—like a prize, an award—sat in the ashtray before him.

To Oliver's right, beneath a large white umbrella, the would-be swimmer sat alone at a table for three, his upper body now concealed beneath a tasteful sweater. Italian. Expensive. Blue. A cup of coffee was, so far, his only companion. The two empty chairs were deeply shaded, waiting for God-knows-who to arrive. *Probably two more spoilsports. Professionals, no doubt.* There were people like that. Oliver knew this from sad experience. At school, a whole clan had existed of lordly bullies whose lives had been dedicated, so it seemed, to upsetting other people's applecarts.

Oh, well.

Damn. There was the dreaded child.

Oh, yes, of course. They had to be staying in this hotel! Didn't they just. Please don't remember me—please don't recognize me. Don't.

Over time, Oliver had praised God that he was queer. *No children. No children. None.* He himself was the only child he had ever known. No siblings and no playmates. In the street and at school, he had hated all others. *All they do is take*—or so it seemed. *None of them ever gives anything back.* Oddly enough, in his later life, he worshipped the childlike wonders of the artists who were his companions. *They see with divine simplicity,* he had said to René. *They respond to everything with divine simplicity.* Like children—yes—but not.

Now—*and wouldn't you know it*—he had not brought down the magazine he'd been reading. Or the book. Or anywhere else to hide. He would have to brazen it out.

You little devil. Stay away from me ...

Oliver said a prayer for all the cats in Naoussa.

The boy came dangerously close. He was wearing water-wings. Red. *Good. If I can puncture them, maybe he'll drown ...*

Oliver watched as the boy and his father made a rather solemn procession across the stones to a table beneath a distant umbrella. In their wake, a woman carrying towels, a woven raffia bag, a hardcover novel and a pair of sandals followed as if distracted. *Where am I, now?* she seemed to be saying—lifting her tinted glasses and squinting at the world around her. She was blonde, almost statuesque—exquisite. Like the boy's father, she seemed to have been scissored from a magazine.

"*As-tu la Bronzine?*" she said. Oliver waited to see who would answer.

"*Oui,*" said the man, giving the child a playful nudge with his fist. He did not look once at the approaching woman.

"*Et les cigarettes?*"

"*Oui.*"

"*Et* Le Monde?"

"*Oui.*"

And the world? Oliver could not help smiling

Of course, it was only a newspaper, but the way the woman had said the words, she might have meant them literally. *Oh, how tired I am.* That was what her body said, as she reached the table and collapsed into the one remaining empty chair. *What a day! What a night! What a life!*

Oliver's breakfast arrived. It featured a basket of croissants.

Damn!

Well, he would feed the crescent rolls to the birds and save the butter for the cats. The coffee and the juice could be taken *as is*, and the steaming milk by the spoonful—though he would have preferred it blended with the coffee at the source. And maybe one cube of sugar. A person had to live, after all. Or try.

The boy was afraid of the water. His father had taken him over to the pool after their breakfast had been ordered, and hunkered down beside him. They were right at the edge and the man had his arm around the child's waist.

Oliver could see the tears, but he couldn't hear the words—only voices—mostly the father's, sweetly cajoling, smiling, confident. *If only my father had been like that, I wouldn't have ended up hydrophobic myself ...* Oliver could remember all too distinctly the feeling of being lifted bodily and thrown down with such force that he sank to the bottom. His father had been ashamed of Oliver's tears and cries. Boys should not be like that. Boys should be brave. They should jump right in at the deep end and come up shouting *hurrah!*

Oliver lighted another cigarette. The father had climbed down into the pool. He and the boy were at the shallow end and the water barely reached the man's calves. He was showing the child how delightful the water was—what fun it was to be wet and to splash about like a dolphin.

"*Non.*"

"*Oui, mon cher. Oui? Pour Papa?*"

The man's hands reached towards his son, their fingers beckoning.

"*Non.*"

The boy's face had taken on an expression more often found on a woman's face when she is holding out for the final enticement. Any minute now, the answer would be *oui*—but not yet.

"*Alain?*"

It was the mother. The wife. The man turned.

"*Les repas arrivent.*"

The waiter bringing their breakfast had almost reached their table. The man, leaning forward, placed his hands on the edge of the pool and hoisted himself from the water. The top of Oliver's tongue made its way onto his upper lip. It was inadvertent. Automatic. The sight of a man's wet body, gleaming in the sun.

Oliver narrowed his eyes. He really should look away. René had been gone for only a month. *Besides, he's a married man, with a child, and …*

"*Au secours! Au secours!*"

Alain had taken no more than three steps away, with his back to the child. And the child was thrashing in the water.

The waiter, having deposited the tray, turned in the cry's direction. The mother stood up. The man with the yellow bathing cap put down his cup. Alain, the father, went running. Oliver pushed back his chair.

"Au secours! Au secours!"

Alain was now in the water and lifting the boy to his breast. Oliver heard some indecipherable words of comfort and drew his chair back to the table. Alain was exiting the pool, the child still held in his arms. Oliver muttered: "the silly twit couldn't possibly have drowned. He's wearing water-wings."

How children do love causing a panic. Roaring *au secours* and splashing up a storm. Anything for attention. Anything. Even pretending ... *it. The D-word.*

Now, of course, he'll eat a lovely breakfast and go off into the bushes and kill something. Something that won't be able to cry for help, because the child's hands will be around its neck.

C'est la-bloody-vie, right? C'est la-bloody-vie.

Oliver's life had always been in the theatre. Not as an actor—*never that*—but as a property-maker. He was extremely skilled and very well thought of. He worked for the Opera and for the Ballet at Covent Garden. That was where he'd met René, who had been a costume-cutter. Not a designer—*never that*—but having contact with the materials and cutting out the shapes of gods. Oliver's forte was hand-props—the ceremonial knives for the suicide of *Madama Butterfly*—the stick-masks for *Romeo and Juliet*—the two-edged sword of *Siegfried*. This was the music he sang and hummed and roared in his mind: Puccini, Prokofiev, Wagner.

Sitting in front of all his uneaten food, he wondered how he might manage to transport the butter for his cats. The crescent rolls were simple. He took each one in hand and crumbled it into a handkerchief spread in his lap.

Butter. It would melt in his pocket. It would stain his trousers. The cats would have to live without it.

Someone else had arrived. An elderly woman who wore what appeared to be an evening gown, and who was accompanied by a young woman in her twenties. The dowager carried herself with exemplary poise, the poise abetted by a walking-stick—the stick as slim as the figure it supported. The gown, a sort of morning coat, was a deep shade of purple with silver facings. The silver was echoed in the slippers, whose toes could be seen when the woman sat down. She sat in the deepest shade—at the farthest distance—beneath the umbrella previously raised exclusively above the would-be swimmer. As she entered, he rose—and nodded.

"Good morning."

English. Not American.

Well—a person can't always be right.

Clearly, the would-be swimmer provided whatever physical attentions Madam required. A gigolo, perhaps—most certainly her lover.

The one thing I've never done—the one thing I never considered. Never. Buying love. Sex—not love. It wasn't sex I loved—it was having René's arms about me. A presence—not a body.

The younger woman was obviously an employee—perhaps a secretary. She was modest before the man, even shy, acknowledging his presence with nothing more than a nod before she sat and began to eat in silence.

Only Madam clattered her utensils. Her hands were unsteady—her fingers, ring-encrusted, were gnarled and arthritic. And yet there was not a trace of age in her face. Oliver judged there had been so many face lifts, she must be incapable of expression. Her hair was thinning—in places almost to the point of baldness. Its colour was pale as the juice of a strawberry left in the bottom of a champagne glass.

"*Au secours! Au secours!* "

Oliver turned towards the pool. *Not again.*

"*Au secours! Au secours!* "

Alain was on his feet. Madam looked up from her eggs. The stroke survivor picked up the yellow ball and swivelled in his chair.

"*Au secours! Au secours!* "

The pool was absolutely empty of anything but water.

The small boy's mother rose from her chair and moved towards the edge of the terrace that overlooked the bay. There was the mosque—implacable. There were the breeze-rippled stretches of sea. There were the gulls, out floating on the air. There were the tumbled walls and the stony flats. But not a sign of her son.

Oliver decided it was only proper to rise and join the hunt.

"*Au secours! Au secours!* "

Damn. In rising, he spilled his handkerchief of crumbled crescent rolls. Also, he stubbed his sandalled toe on a table leg. *Damn—damn—damn, you little monster!*

Alain and his wife moved closer together in order to consult each other's sense of where the cry was coming from. Oliver could hear their voices, but the only word he recognized was the woman's name: *Christiane.* She waved her arms out over the bay.

Rien! She turned and waved them over the terrace. *Rien!* The pool. *Rien!* And then, to Oliver's horror, she started to beat her fists on her husband's chest.

Oliver crossed the terrace, moving to the left of the open-air bar that was there beneath an awning of its own. No bartender yet— still too early.

"*Au secours!* "

Then laughter.

Oliver turned back.

There were the water-wings—or, at least, their tiny fins— waving below the counter of the bar.

Oliver leaned in.

The boy was waiting for him, and threw a dish rag, wetted, up into his face.

Oliver, astonished, fell back. The dish rag hung from his nose, a grotesque parody of a cream pie in a silent comedy. He pulled it away and stood there, nearly in tears. The child—*oh, wouldn't he just!*—stared up at him, pointed, and screamed with laughter.

Christiane, having seen that the child was alive, and having realized she had been duped into panic, turned on her heel and marched down the wide stone steps to the first of the descending flats below the terrace. Alain came over to the bar.

He looked at Oliver and closed his eyes and gave a despairing sigh. Clearly, he could think of nothing to say.

Oliver did not wait for the man to collect his wits. He simply rolled the dish rag into a ball and handed it to him without a word. Then he walked away. The rest of the day was spent in Naoussa.

———————

There is a plane tree in the centre of the village, around which a number of bars and cafés are clustered. This is not where the chairs all face the sea, but where tourists wait for public transport and buy their postcards.

The plane tree must be greatly old. Its roots reach out in a circle of visible protuberances that might have been designed as a compass, so perfect is their distribution. At some time—maybe as long ago as fifty or sixty years—someone decided to build a stone-walled container for the roots, filling it with earth and covering the earth with a thin layer of cement. The roots of the plane tree ride above this surface, twisting in unison—a school of dolphins in a plaster sea.

Mid-afternoon on the day of the dish-rag episode, Oliver was seated at a table dappled with leafy shade beneath the arms of the tree. He was very slightly *tiddly*—having drunk a litre of rosé since noon. *Tiddly*—his own word—and sad. Everyone around him was so alive—so beautiful—so busy and so perfectly paired with some-one else alive and beautiful and busy that Oliver wanted to weep.

Of course, *a person with self-respect never weeps in public.* Even in the minutes following René's demise, Oliver had kept his tears at bay. None of the doctors—none of the orderlies—none of the nurses—witnessed a moment's lapse in his self-control. And when he had walked from the hospital with René's possessions in a suit-case and René's raincoat over his arm, he had looked like a man who might have been going to visit his mother—not a man who was going home to telephone the crematorium.

But now there were all these people—and all this life—and

there were doves above Oliver's head and seabirds screeching in the harbour—and it was almost unbearable.

Gone.

No coming back. No reappearance. No more leaning down in the lamplight: *what are you reading now?* No more toes touching toes beneath the sheets. No more Dunhill cologne in the bathroom. No more linking of arms or holding of hands. No more *what's for supper?* No more *ta, my darlin'.* No more "*Somewhere Over the Rainbow*" sung off-key. No more rainbows. No more songs. Just gone. Into dust.

Oliver ordered another half-litre of rosé. *So what? Other people get pissed in the afternoon. I've got rights and reasons, same as anyone.*

Waiting, he looked at the dogs collected beneath the tree. It seemed to be a given that, every day at this hour, the dogs would gather there and take their siesta in one another's company. Whose they were and even if they had names and homes was not at all clear. They looked well fed enough, but none of them had a collar or any other mark of human identification. Perhaps, like the cats, they fed from the public purse of café tidbits. On Paros, almost anything could live beneath the sky, so long as there was a food supply.

The wine came. Oliver poured the first glass. *I don't care what it costs. I'm going to spend every penny I've saved—every penny we saved—and have a decent, human holiday. I've got my job—and something of my health—and rights and reasons besides.* He drank.

It was curious. The light had shifted—revealing what looked like pock-marks in the cement beneath the tree.

Oliver squinted.

Not, of course, pock-marks—but what?

Cat-prints and dog-prints—that's what it was. Cat-prints, dog-prints and child-prints—the child-prints barefooted. Fifty—sixty years old. Here today and gone tomorrow. *This is my mark that tells you I was here.*

I. Me. I.

Oliver looked away.

How could he bear it? Everyone—everyone gone. Or going. Nothing but footprints left behind. Nothing but: *this is my mark ...*

There was the child.

The dreaded one himself. And his father, Alain. They were walking hand in hand, and beyond them, hidden as always behind her tinted glasses, Christiane—with a canvas bag that looked to be weighted down with tissued parcels. Clothing, more than likely. The shops were excellent here. There were even local couturiers, whose cottonwear was downright splendid.

Oliver cringed. *Must you be everywhere?*

The boy broke free and ran out onto the cement surround of the tree. The dogs looked up, alarmed. Two of them, seeming to have recognized an enemy by instinct, rose and came down amidst the tables. The others sat and watched, wary of the boy but willing to take their chances until he made an overtly aggressive move.

The boy looked down and saw the paw-prints.

"Papa!"

Alain moved closer, standing at the edge of the stone circle. The boy pointed. *"Les chiens anciens!"*

Alain smiled. *"Oui. Et les chats aussi."*

The boy looked again. His expression altered. *How did one reconcile this?* it said. *"Papa?"*

"Oui."

"*Les enfants anciens. Oui? Regards.*"

By now, Christiane had caught up with them and stood beside her husband.

The child, who had still not been accorded his name, lifted one foot and then the other, removing his shoes.

Oliver, unacknowledged and perhaps unseen, watched with astonishment as the monster-child all at once took up a position that might have been copied from an ancient frieze. Raising his shoes like bunches of grapes above his head, he assumed a pose not unlike Nijinsky dancing *L'Après-midi d'un faun*—and stepped out, wading in the dusty footprints of whatever child, however long ago, had danced before him through the wet cement.

He danced in slow motion—all the dogs entranced. And all the people. "*Papa! Papa! Maman! Maman! Après moi! Après moi!*" He held out his hands—not stopping, but dancing on.

Alain climbed onto the compass, reaching back for Christiane's hand. He was smiling. She was not. But they waited there together until their child had made his way once more around the tree— and then all three together made the circle, dipping and rising and stepping to unheard music.

Nobody stirred but the dancers beneath the tree. All were transfixed. Oliver could barely breathe.

And then they were gone.

The child had begun to run—and his parents with him—the child with his shoes above him, clapping them like cymbals, and the air behind him filled with his laughter. And his cry.

"*Suivez! Suivez! Suivez-moi!*"

Follow. Follow. Follow me.

———————

Some hours and another litre of rosé later, as the evening darkened, Oliver was forced to engage a taxi to bring him home.

The taxi driver held him upright in the lift and walked him along the corridor to his room. Oliver paid him and thanked him and sent him away.

On the bureau there was a bottle of ouzo—meant to have been kept as a souvenir. Still very much in the sway of the day's rosé, Oliver somehow got the cap off the bottle and poured a full and nearly lethal glass of liquor. Dragging a chair to the open balcony doorway, he then sat down and raised his glass at the moon.

Now, I will drink and smoke myself to death. Who would care? It couldn't matter less. I will drink and smoke myself to death and there will be a memorial service at Covent Garden, where Maureen Forrester and Jessye Norman will sing the flower duet from Butterfly *above my casket, scattering all those cherry blossoms it took me a month to create by hand around their kimonos, cut by René, designed by Tanya Moiseiwitsch, directed by Jonathan Miller, while the Queen and Prince Philip look on from the Royal Box and Pavarotti sobs in the wings ...*

The moon was descending. Late, late. An early-morning moon—the rarest moon of all. And all the stars above the sea—and the sea the colour of René's eyes ... *and I—I will sit here until I ...*

Sleep.

The next day, Oliver did not appear on his balcony until ninethirty.

He had so long been sober—fifteen or twenty years—that having a hangover might have been something experienced by aliens. He could barely move without the reverberations striking the inside rim of his skull with hammer-blows. Nothing—not even standing perfectly still—was of any help. He held the iron railing before him, begging it to hold him upright. Above him, the sky was ablaze with cruel light. Closing his eyes, Oliver sank down into a chair. Breakfast—for all that it would be only a glass of juice and a caffe latte—would have to wait. Perhaps until it was lunchtime. Teatime. Or supper. He could no more contemplate eating than joining a brass band. Everything was pounding. Everything.

And below him, somewhere on the terrace, somewhere near the pool, a voice was calling.

Au secours!

Oliver descended.

Alain and Christiane were nowhere to be seen. Only the dowager with her gigolo—or whatever—and the stroke survivor.

Au secours ...

The words were in Oliver's mind. The air was still and, far away, the calls of gulls could be heard over the bay. Beyond the mosque on its island, a yacht with limp white sails was riding, almost stilled—its people lying in the sun.

Au secours.

Where?

Oliver wandered, sliding his feet along the stones so as not to jar his system. Of course, it would be the dreaded child who forced him to move, when all he wanted was to lie on his bed.

"Au secours!"

Now, it was spoken aloud. Shouted from below the terrace. Screamed. *You little rotter! Shut up!*

Oliver said nothing. He scouted for the water-wings, seeing them at last, where the boy crouched throwing pebbles into a shallow pool of water.

Oliver clambered down the steps—his skull ringing like *The Anvil Chorus.*

The child's back was to him.

The words *au secours* had become a kind of song—tuneless, but sung with wavering intensity.

Oliver spoke in French.

"Boy," he said. "I have come to tell you something."

Hearing the voice of an unexpected adult so close by, the boy's face registered alarm as he turned to see who was there.

They squinted at each other.

Oliver sat down.

He was calm—he was succinct. He wasted no time and he spoke with what he imagined was a friendly tone. Or relatively so. He knew the boy did not like him and, certainly, he did not like the boy. One bit. But he intended to have his say and bring the maddening irritation of *au secours* to an end.

There was once a little shepherd boy, he began. And told the whole story, all the way to its gruesome conclusion, of "The Boy Who Cried Wolf."

As the child crouched, listening, he threw the last of his pebbles into the pool and dusted his hands. In Aesop's fable, the boy cried *wolf* again and again when there was no wolf to endanger his sheep. Everyone came running in response to his cries—hurrying up the hillside from the town below. This, the boy enjoyed. So much excitement. So many people. So much importance. At last, however, once it was clear there was no wolf—when time and time again they had hurried to the rescue all for nothing—the people gave up responding to his cries. They turned in their beds and went back to sleep.

And then—can you guess what happened?

A wolf appeared in the moonlight one night—a very hungry wolf.

Of course, the boy cried: *Wolf! Wolf,* he cried, over and over. *WOLF!*

But no one came. They had heard it all before—gone running once too often to believe the boy that night.

And so …

The child was wide-eyed. Silenced. Enchanted.

"*Au secours,*" he whispered.

"No," said Oliver. "No one could save him. No one could save the sheep. All were slaughtered and dragged away by morning—and only the shepherd's crook was left behind to tell what had become of the flock and of the boy who cried *wolf.*"

He waited.

What would happen?

Without a word, the child stood up and left him.

Oliver did not move.

Done, he prayed. *Over.*

Out in the bay, a breeze had lifted. Two of the figures lying on the yacht got to their feet and went to attend to their sails.

Oliver waved.

Someone waved back.

Oliver sighed. He almost wept, not knowing why. The boy, his face attentive at last—its features softened? The blue, like René's eyes? The gulls high up above him? What could it be?

All he knew was, he had not waved at anyone—stranger or friend—since René had passed.

Oliver went upstairs to rest.

On the second floor, he sat in a chair and paused to catch his breath. He was not in good shape—too much sitting about in hospitals and at the work-bench in the properties department. Too many wolves. Too many cries for help. Too many cigarettes. Too much wine. He should have taken the lift.

Some distance down the corridor to his right he could hear someone speaking what appeared to be a monologue. There must, for whatever reason, be an open doorway. Slowly, as he stood there, Oliver surmised the voice belonged to Christiane. She was crying. Not in the sobbing sense, but weeping as she spoke—all her words liquified by tears.

Oliver could not hear well enough to tell what she said—but he knew it must be addressed to Alain. He also knew the subject was despair—knowing this because the tone of her voice was the very same as the voice inside his own being. *Being*—yes. *Not* head. *Not* mind. Inside my *being*.

Christiane was mourning. Mourning the loss of all hope—and the loss of all possible happiness. She was consigning herself and perhaps her son and husband to—what? To what? To eternal desolation? Maybe that was why Oliver had waved to that stranger.

Not *hello*—but *goodbye*. To everything. Oh, don't say that. It can't—I won't let it be true.

At last, Christiane was finished.

There was a silence—broken only by a single cough that must have come from Alain. And then, Alain himself appeared. He was wearing shorts and a pale blue polo shirt. He carried a tennis racket and a yellow net full of balls. He moved along the corridor without a sound. It was doubtful he was even aware of Oliver's presence. His expression was fixed. He went down the stairs at a steady but unhurried pace. When he was gone—and just before Oliver rose to continue his own progress—the door, which had been open, closed. Not with a slam, but only with a *click*. A period, not an exclamation point. Oliver thought it was the sound of all things ending—the same, the very same, as the gentle *click* he had heard when the nurse leaned down to turn off René's monitors.

At five o'clock, Oliver was lying on a chaise in the shade. He wore his bathing suit and had spread a towel across his face. The pool lay placid beyond his feet. He had slept on his bed and again on the chaise. He was in a state of drift. A glass of wine began to float into view—now not threatening, as the thought of wine had been all morning. Now—a restorative. Now—a tonic. A renewed delight ...

"*Au secours!*"

Oh, God! Not again.

"*Au secours! Au secours!*"

There was a burst of distant splashing. The childish ruse

augmented with sound effects. Stage directions, plus libretto! *Next thing, he'll ask for props!*

"Monsieur! Monsieur!"

Piss off, you little bitch. I warned you not to do this—and I thought you'd understood.

Oliver stuffed the corners of the towel into his ears. For once, it would be pleasant to bear the burden of René's deafness. *Wouldn't it be loverly?* He wouldn't have to hear the rotten child at all. And after going to all the trouble of telling Aesop's fable in French? *In French, my dear! The precocious pig!*

"Au secours! Au secours!"

That was better. Barely audible.

Ten minutes later, Oliver gauged that the child must have given up his game and gone in search of Alain and Christiane. There was not a sound.

Good.

He withdrew the plugs from his ears and pulled the towel—it was red—down onto his chest. There above him was the sky beyond the leaves of an acacia tree.

Far, far away, at a height he could not surmise, a large white bird was floating on an updraught. Albatross.

Are you swimming there—swimming? he who had never swum said to the bird.

Then he sat up.

There was not a soul in sight. Even the waitress had left the outdoor bar. She often did this late in the afternoon. People then went up to their rooms to shower and bathe. It was now five-thirty.

Oliver pushed his toes into his sandals and pulled his cotton sweater over his head. He would have the rosé in town, he decided. The walk would do him good.

He made his way around the pool—avoiding the bar, for fear the brat might be lying in wait with another dish rag. *The devil. One day, I'll laugh about it, no doubt—but not now.*

Where Christiane, Alain and the child were normally to be found, the chairs and the chaise beneath the cotton shade were vacant. Christiane had left a magazine behind. *Vogue.* And a tube of Bronzine. Also, the water-wings.

There they sat, not unlike a cartoon manifestation of lungs. Red. Red and shining.

Au secours.

This was not a cry. It was just the words presenting themselves in Oliver's mind. *Au secours.*

He stared at the water-wings.

He felt ill.

Don't.

But he had to. He had to turn around and look.

The child—just the shape of him—lay in a curled position on the bottom of the pool where it was deepest.

Oliver fell to his knees. He knew there was nothing he could do. He couldn't even swim. *Wolf,* he heard himself whisper. But his voice, like his sense of reality, had quite deserted him.

In the morning, Oliver sat in his place immobilized and barely breathing. He was numb. They all were—all the staff and all the guests. There was not a word.

Children should not die like that. They shouldn't die at all. Death is for adults—persons who have lived.

Oliver looked across at the man with the yellow ball, who sat disconsolate as all the rest. The dowager, the gigolo, the demure secretary and all the other unidentified, unidentifiable figures. Young and old. Old and young. But none—not one of them a child.

Passed. Departed. Left.

But, no. Not *left*. God-damn it—*dead*.

There. He had said it.

Earlier—perhaps at eight A.M. or nine—Oliver had watched as Christiane and Alain took their leave of the hotel. They had walked through the lobby hand in hand. Christiane, at last, had removed her tinted glasses. A remarkably beautiful woman, without a trace of expression on her face. A numbed mask of anguish, nothing more.

Alain shook hands with the hotel manager. Whatever arrangements had been required had been made and acted upon. The body of the boy had gone on before them to the larger town of Paros. Perhaps from there, they would take a plane to Athens. Or whatever. Whatever it is that people do when they suffer a tragedy away from home.

Oliver had been particularly heartened to see them holding onto one another—Alain, Christiane—Christiane, Alain—with such tenacity. For however long, they would be united now—and maybe, somehow, they would survive their loss intact.

On the terrace, their image wavered in Oliver's memory—their backs like the backs of disappearing angels fading into the mist of a daydream. Already, they were unreal. Their lives with their son might have been a cautionary tale and nothing more. A fable by Aesop, told by Oliver Sher to a child. *And all the people in the town below the hill turned over in their beds and went back to sleep ...*

Oliver sighed.

Later in the afternoon he sat beneath the acacia tree and stared at the pale hotel. How beautiful it was—and white. Like the mosque on the island in the bay. Oliver stood up and went to look out over the water. That morning's yacht was anchored there, its sails pulled down, its canvas awning spread above the poop-deck. A small group of people sat together in the shade. *I waved to one of those.*

Behind him, Oliver heard the familiar sound of the yellow ball as it hit the surface of the pool. He turned.

The man in the bathing cap stood at the edge of the water, his toes hooked over the stones.

"I want to," he said. "But I can't."

At last he had spoken. *English.*

Oliver did not understand. He had seen the man swimming. What could he mean: *I can't?* Perhaps the death of the child by drowning had intimidated him.

"Did you speak?"

"I'm sorry. I didn't mean to disturb you."

"No, no," said Oliver. "You didn't disturb me. I was only looking out at the sea. And I was wondering ..."

"Yes?"

"Do you mind my asking? Have you, perhaps ... I mean—have you suffered a stroke?"

"Well, now. I don't mind your asking. But what makes you think so?"

Oliver gestured. "The ball," he said.

The man put his hands behind him. He moved his toes and rocked back and forth on the stones. When he finally spoke, he seemed more alone than when he had been silent. The voice was barely audible.

"I had a dog," he said. "A dog. It died."

Oliver bit his lip. And waited.

"Kip," the man said. "Kipper."

Oliver nodded.

"He was old, of course—and age will have its way. But ... fourteen years we had together."

"Yes."

"Fourteen years and two months."

"I see."

There was the slightest pause. And then: "have you ever lived with a dog?"

"Only when I was a child," said Oliver. "A kid. I had an Irish terrier."

The man said nothing. He nodded.

They both looked over at the yellow ball. It had floated into the centre of the pool.

The man rocked back and forth again—and stopped. "This was our game," he said. "Do you see? He loved it when I threw the ball. And ... if there was water ..." He paused. "He was a water spaniel. Bred especially, you know. Bred for retrieving birds. Birds that had been shot. Ducks, you see. Geese. Mostly ducks." Another pause. "I never asked him to do that. Never. Of course. Nothing dead. Never. Only the ball. I wouldn't know how to kill, you see. Anything. Nothing. I don't ... I simply can't imagine it. How is it done? How can people do that? Take a life for sport?"

"I've never known. Don't know. I feel the same as you, I think."

"Kip died of cancer. In his stomach. I had him put down. I had to do it. The suffering was unbearable to watch, you see. And so ..."

René.

There was a silence. Seconds. Minutes. Bird-song.

The dowager rose and left with her retinue. A funeral cortège.

But then: "what a lovely evening," she said. "What a lovely, *lovely* evening."

Turning, she raised her arm at the sky. "Look. Oh, look," she said, "at the sun." She might have been waving to it: *goodbye: hello.*

Oliver glanced at the yellow ball. And the shadow of the child beneath it—unerased and unerasable.

He would buy a dog. That's what. He would buy a dog—and life would go on, from death to death.

And tonight, he would eat—shrimps and a chicken souvlaki. With a salad on the side.

Kellerman's Windows

1

KELLERMAN STOOD in the open window, his elbows braced against the sill. He couldn't sleep. His body would not lie down. His eyes would not close.

Midnight—July—and all the rooftops of Paris were spread out before him, every one of them a stepping stone to the next. Kellerman had always thought this. *With a running start, you could leap from rooftop to rooftop all the way to the moon.* He'd said so to Shirley: *look at them out there! You want to play hopscotch? Bring your stones and bring your chalk; leave your worries on the doorstep ...*

She was asleep now, curled on the bed in the room behind him, her wine glass half emptied on the table beside her. *I'm tired, Marty. Tired. I can't play games tonight.*

It didn't matter. She was there.

Kellerman turned again to the window, his wine glass in hand, the bottle on the sill. Looking out at the slated roofs and the sky, he felt like a child who had just unwrapped a gift and the gift was exactly what he'd hoped it would be.

A rooftop! A chimney!

He drank.

"Here is where it all began," he said. Not so loud that Shirley would hear him, only so he could hear himself. "I'm alive—the same as I was before." he said. Alive and in Paris staring out at its beloved skyline. *In my time, fifty years ago, every young man's dream began out there beyond this window. Paris. Women. Fame.*

Name one who would not be Hemingway.

Can't. It's what we all wanted, back then. So, I might not be Hemingway. But I am me. Martin Kellerman—who made his own way and became his own writer.

He set the glass down, careful not to let it tip, and lighted a cigarette. *Lethal, who cares? Smoke and Paris—the stink of Gauloise everywhere—the stink, the smell, the scent, the perfume of them.*

"Wonderful!" Aloud.

He blew a cloud and waved his hand in it. *Smoke and Paris go together like smoke and mirrors.* Haussmann's incantation. Haussmann, the city planner. Haussmann, the magician. *Paris? I'll give you Paris. Ta-dah!*

Kellerman poured more Côtes du Rhone, enjoying the heft of the bottle as he tipped its mouth to the glass. Its weight, in itself, was a pleasure:—*not yet empty*, it told him.

Yes. It was a good thing he had done—was doing. Coming back to the beginning, nearing the end. One more book to finish. One more triumph. And Shirley with him. With him still, in spite of twenty-six years of tumultuous marriage—glorious—ghastly—tender and terrible times. Three children. Fourteen books. High on the lists. Low on staying power. *You'll have to run faster, Marty,* his publisher had said. *Sure. Nothing to it!* And then, one day: *I can't run any more.* The words not coming. The mind refusing. The body not responding—turning on him, just when he needed it most. *Give me a rest,* he'd said. And this was it. Paris and rejuvenation.

"Marty? Come to bed." Shirley's voice was almost a whisper.

"Can't," he said. "Go back to sleep."

"You all right?"

"Fine. Just fine."

"You know what the doctor said."

"Sure. He said to my mother: *Mrs Kellerman, you have a healthy baby boy! Rejoice!*"

Shirley snorted and turned in the bed. "Your mother had five healthy babies, Marty. The other four are all dead."

"Go to sleep."

"Yes, sir. Yes, sir. Anything you say." She was already going, drifting back towards her dreams; her breathing deepening, her fingers uncurling, letting go—her left leg reaching for the bottom of the bed. With a sigh, she left him.

Kellerman turned again to the window and drank more wine. *To hell with what the doctor said. I'm alive. I'm living.*

2

He could not believe it. Forty-six years ago—almost half a century—Kellerman had stood in this very same room, watching the very same skyline.

Nothing changes. Everything changes. Everything the same and everything different.

All those windows out there glowing—luminescent in the dark—were the same as he had seen when he was twenty, but all the lives beyond them would be different now. Many deaths and many births—leave-takings—arrivals—changing circumstances ... *There, for instance.* One storey down, across the street, an old woman stood in the middle of her living-room, staring at a photograph.

She must have been seventy-five or eighty—her pure white hair pushed back and away from her face. She wore a pale blue wrapper and a high-necked gown. All around her, the tabletops were cluttered with mementos—other photographs in frames, empty vases, porcelain figures, cut-glass goblets, one bronze horse.

The woman kissed the picture in her hand and held it then against her breast. Perhaps her dead husband. Perhaps a child. Turning, she gazed into a distant corner. *There?* she seemed to say.

No.

She turned again and fixed her sights on a shelf containing books and Indo-Chinese dolls.

There?

Perhaps.

She crossed the room with a swaying motion, almost dancing, threading her way between the tables and chairs. At the shelf, she removed some books and put the picture in their place. Stepping away, she looked at what she had done.

No. It was wrong. One too many faces staring back at her. She snatched up the photograph and passed from sight, only to reappear in the dining-room, whose windows, unlike the others, were closed.

It took her no time at all to make her final decision.

There.

The photograph, which Kellerman of course could not decipher, had been set between two candlesticks on a gaming table whose polished lid had been raised against the wall.

Perfect. Perfection.

The past was now complete—and in its place.

The old woman made for her decanters on the sideboard. Wine was for the daytime. Midnight wanted Cognac.

3

Kellerman heard voices directly opposite. Two people—both unseen—were having an argument. Every window was opened wide in what appeared to be a very large apartment.

The wrangling moved from room to room. Accusations! Denials! Threats and counter-threats! All with such vivid articulation. Kellerman thought of waking Shirley just to hear the words. All the words for rage and hurt. All the words for infidelity and shame—and all the words like breaking plates, hurled into the night. Much about betrayal, everything about love. And then the final *never again. JAMAIS!* And slamming doors. All the usual—all too familiar—but, this time, spoken by two men.

Kellerman could hardly breathe. He felt as if he had taken part in the argument himself. He closed his eyes and, when he opened them, one of the couple across the street had come to the window. He stood there staring down. Seconds later, the other appeared below. He did not look up. Instead, he slung a jacket over his shoulder, took a few steps to the corner and was gone.

Kellerman didn't move. He knew he would not be seen. The abandoned lover in the window opposite was blind with self-absorption. In all the world there was only one other person—and he had disappeared.

Kellerman watched. The man, though balding, was young—perhaps no more than twenty-seven, twenty-eight. What hair remained was short-cropped and red and the head it revealed was turned towards the sky—*as if some passing angel would tell him what to do.*

As if some passing angel ...

Robert's invention. Robert's game.

As if some passing angel would teach me how to dance.

As if some passing angel would drop a million-dollar bill.

As if some passing angel would ...

Tell me what to do.

Robert was their only son and the only one of their children who was gay. *Gay*—a word that Kellerman detested, but a word that Robert had worn with pride.

What's wrong with *homosexual*?

Nothing, Dad. It's just not cool.

What's *gay* about being kicked to death?

No answer. Robert was dead—the victim of gay-bashing. Skinheads.

Well. At least it's over now.

Kellerman watched the young man turn and walk away. As he watched, something impelled him—perhaps some passing angel—to whisper: *don't get "lost in the jungle."* Another of Robert's inventions. His last and favourite game.

4

To Kellerman's right, beyond the intersection, he could see the Hotel Luxembourg. Its windows were slowly going dark, since now it was well past midnight. Travellers, dazed with jet-lag, bed down early. Still, one set of windows, two storeys shy of his own, was lit. In one of these, a young man sat transfixed, gazing out at the street. He was smoking a cigarette and drinking wine. Kellerman's *doppelgänger*.

Beyond this young man, the room was blue with the flickering light of a television set. Through the second window, Kellerman could see a bed and, on the bed, a dishevelled young woman propped up with pillows. She was sucking a strand of her own dark hair and staring vacantly at what was on the screen. Because of the heat, she had thrown back the sheet, revealing her naked legs. One bare foot beat time to music Kellerman could barely hear.

Doppelgänger poured more wine into his glass from a bottle taken from the sill beside him. Kellerman thought: *it's me, forty-six years ago, with all my dreams intact. Paris. Women. Fame. And lying in between the shirts and underwear in my suitcase was a manuscript half written that was going to take the world by storm.*

He could see all this—he could read it in the young man's shoulders pushing forward into the dark above the street—in the tilt of his head as he measured out the distances between the roofs. *The rooftops of Paris—out there waiting. Stepping stones all the way to the moon.* And the moon shining down, its aureole touching the city of light.

Bring your stones and bring your chalk, leave your worries on the doorstep ...

Now he was back—with another manuscript half written that would take the world by storm, if only his god-damned publisher would give him time.

5

Kellerman turned away from the window.

Shirley?

She was fast asleep, her breathing gentle and steady. The only sign of tension was the grip she had on the piece of Kleenex in her hand. *My clutch*, she called it. She carried them everywhere—even into the shower, where Kellerman would find them wedged like velvet stones between the liquid soap and the shampoo.

Shirley. Guide and companion—vexing—mysterious—filled

with laughter and loaded for action—going to do battle with every kind of darkness, her own and his. And Robert's, in the grave. Mother of three—enraged and stricken with grief that would never end—endowed with boundless astonishment in the face of daughters whose wonders had no limit. Rachel. Miranda. And all their brood.

Kellerman paused on his way to the bathroom and looked down into Shirley's face. *I got me a lioness,* he thought. *What do you think of that, Mister Hemingway! A lioness—and I didn't fire a shot!*

Kissing his fingertips, he laid them against her lips, and like a child with its parents' hand, she kissed them back without waking.

In the bathroom, Kellerman opened a second bottle of Côtes du Rhone and, drinking from its mouth, he toasted himself in the mirror.

"Hello," he whispered. "Welcome back." And took the bottle through the bedroom's darkness to the window.

6

Down below him, the Cognac Widow was dusting and polishing her treasures.

You're mad, dear lady! It's one o'clock in the morning!

And there was music.

What?

He couldn't tell, but it was coming from her windows—her dining-room windows now standing open with the rest. Not a waltz, but a jagged tango, to which she moved with duster in one hand, glass in the other—partnered by ghosts, applauded by dolls and photographs and one bronze horse—her empty vases sprouting flowers and all the cut-glass goblets overflowing with champagne.

Lighting the last of the Gauloise, Kellerman leaned against the window frame, his hip pressed into the sill.

Two bottles of Côtes du Rhone and one whole package of cigarettes.

Well, no. He had shared the first bottle with Shirley. There was her half-empty glass to prove it. And surely these were yesterday's cigarettes—a partial package only—ten at the most. Or twelve.

Whatever. Certainly this was the last of them.

He focused on the Hotel Luxembourg.

Am I still there?

Yes.

Doppelgänger, shirtless now, had risen to his feet and was leaning far out into the night. His head turned upwards, he twisted towards the sky and took a deeply contented breath. Kellerman watched it filling the young man's chest and heard him exhale.

From the bed, the woman called to him: "for God's sake—aren't you ever coming in?"

No—not yet. Don't. Stay out here under the moon. You will never, never, have this moment again. It has to last you all your life ...

Kellerman himself leaned out.

Kellerman—forty-six years on.

And all the rooftops of Paris spread out before him.

With a running start, he could leap from one to the other all the way to the moon.

When he fell to the floor, he thought he must have tripped mid-flight. The last thing he said was: *damn.* But Shirley didn't hear him. She was sitting with her children in her dream.

7

In the morning, when she found him, he was lying on the carpet with the open window above him and his pyjamas soaked in red wine.

Shirley sat down beside him and took his hand. Closing his eyes, she kissed him and tidied his hair and did up the buttons over his heart and took his hand again.

Done. And well done.

Not a shock. No surprise. It had been half expected. Truth to tell, it was why they had come.

Abracadaver

I RARELY FLY FIRST CLASS and, when I do, it is because a client has bought my ticket. On this occasion, however, I said to myself: *you are seventy-one years old, Vanessa, and you may never get to Paris again. Break the bank and enjoy yourself while you can.*

It is curious. I have money, but spending it alarms me. Because my clients are very often millionaires several times over, I have witnessed every kind of spending a person can imagine. Millionaires are notoriously stingy, but when it comes to travel, clothing and motorcars, they go first class all the way.

On the other hand, how many times have I had to argue the cost of my designs for their gardens? *Oh, we can't have pine trees there! We can't afford pine trees!* And: *isn't that rather a lot of stone work? Do you think you could consider less?*

No.

I win, most often. Except on this one occasion. On the way to revisit some of the great gardens of France, *Miss Stinge* herself has given in not only to first-class flights, but to first-class hotels, as well. In Paris, the sumptuous Lutétia; in Bordeaux, the glorious Burdigala. And in Antibes, the Hôtel du Cap, where only cash is accepted and even the ghosts are famous.

Speaking of famous, I've had an extraordinary encounter here on the plane. The woman across the aisle was tantalizingly familiar, but I wasn't able to place her. An aging film star? A famous author? Must be nearly eighty, but the hair a flaming red and the body almost alarmingly thin, encased in black Chanel—the classic suit, white trim, vulgar buttons. She had to be *someone*—but who?

She was having a problem with her sinuses and had just run out of nose drops. I heard her upbraiding the poor, mousy creature beside her for *allowing this to happen. It's your job to see that all my medication is in place.*

I am a seasoned traveller and, although I have no mousy companion to do for me, I never fail to carry two of everything.

"Madame?"

"Oh—yes—what is it?" She said this with some irritation.

"I happen to have an unopened bottle of nose drops which I would be more than glad to offer." I had already retrieved it from my pocketbook. What I really wanted was to stop the verbal abuse of her companion—*not* to alleviate Madame's discomfort.

Her face lit up. The manner changed completely.

"But—oh!—how very kind you are. Oh, thank you, thank you, thank you." With which, she accepted the bottle, opened it and, hiding behind a handkerchief, applied the drops. Sniffing and snuffling with theatrical panache, she tossed her head from side to side and took great gulps of air. "I can breathe again!"

I smiled and turned away. Her companion was off the hook.

"May I offer you a drink?" she said, a moment later.

The drinks in first class are free. Nonetheless, I accepted her *hospitality*.

"Why, yes," I said. "That would be delightful."

The stewardess appeared.

"What will you have?" said my hostess, turning to me.

"A Virgin Mary."

"One Virgin Mary. And one double vodka martini."

The Mouse gave a small cough.

"Oh, yes," said the woman, "and a ginger ale, no ice."

"Would you care for some salted nuts, Madame Timushka?"

"Absolutely. Almonds."

Timushka.

I blushed. How could I have forgotten? Known to the world by her last name only, Rose-Marie Timushka had been the most famous magician of the last sixty years and more. And doubly famous because she was the only woman who had succeeded in the craft. I saw her when she played New York and again in Boston. Twice. All this before the war. And when the war was over, she had come to Europe and conquered London, Paris, Rome, Madrid. The flaming red hair, the fires that leapt from her finger ends. The clouds of birds that appeared from nowhere. The dismembered man who rose not only to walk again, but to dance. I remember it all as if it were yesterday. The tiny *Mistress of Illusion*, whose height was nothing, but whose stature was immense.

TIMUSHKA!

The Lutétia has its place in history. Its cellars were once the torture chambers of the Gestapo—its corridors crowded with Nazi uniforms. But, when the liberation of Paris was complete in 1944, its honour was restored. The Lutétia became the haven of those released from concentration camps—a hospice for the dying, a home for the homeless whose suffering could barely be imagined.

Today, it is in its glory. The salon unashamedly red, its doormen and its bellhops dressed like cadets, also in red—the lobby reflecting its international prestige with guests of every colour and culture passing through its doors. There is not a language on earth that has not been spoken here. Writers, politicians, film stars, artists and corporate leaders mingle under a single banner: *we are all at the top.* Of course, this is exhilarating—but also somewhat intimidating.

It came as no real surprise when Madame Timushka asked where I was staying, and said: *but I shall be at the Lutétia, too!* As if she would be anywhere else.

At Charles de Gaulle, I was shameless. *Would I care for a ride?* Of course. *Which bags were mine?* Those. *Here comes my driver. Vincent! Miss Van Horne's luggage. This. This. And this.*

The car was a Daimler. I haven't ridden in a Daimler since my stint with the Collier gardens at Newport. And that was thirty years ago!

The Mouse, whose name is Hilda Menzies, sat on the jump seat, holding Timushka's jewel case. I sat beside Madame, with her sables languishing between us. *Yes, it is springtime,* she said, *but I won't go anywhere without them. My old bones chill if there's the slightest draught ...*

And why is she in Paris?

She is publishing her memoirs.

Not an *autobiography*, but *memoirs*.

That is what I call *class*.

Lucky me. My room is one of the best the Lutétia offers—fourth floor and a glorious view of sky, where a large French flag is snapping in the breeze. Down below, I can see the glassed-in roof of the salon. Enchanting.

As I arrived, the chambermaid was hanging fresh towels in the bathroom, singing away as if work itself was a song. Much as I hated to interrupt her, I didn't want her to be embarrassed—so I gave a loud cough to announce my presence.

Instantly, she appeared in the doorway—a sweet, smiling girl, no more than eighteen.

"*Bonjour, madame.*"

We spoke in a mixture of French and English—but the gist of it was this:

"Good day."

"You have had a long journey?"

"Yes. From America. New York."

"Madame is very fortunate. One of France's greatest actors has just vacated this room."

"Oh?"

"Yes. Molyneux."

Molyneux. I was impressed, and told her so. I remember him well. A great romantic.

"He signed my autograph book." She took what appeared to be an artist's sketch-book from the pocket of her apron and showed me his signature. "I always keep this with me," she said, "just in case. So many famous people are guests at the Lutétia."

Molyneux's signature was quite impressive—writ large and with a flourish.

"Are you, perhaps ...?"

"Famous? Oh, my dear child, no!" I laughed.

The girl looked somewhat disappointed.

"It so happens, however," I said, "that I'm about to have a drink in the salon with someone extremely famous. Timushka."

"Oh, madame! The great magician?"

"Yes. And—if you would trust me with your book, I would be delighted to ask for her autograph in your behalf."

She was beaming. "Oh, yes, please, madame! Yes, yes please! How wonderful! My mother speaks of her and the fires she created with her fingertips—and the mystery of the dancing man. Yes, yes! Oh, please!"

When she was gone, I realized I had not asked her name. But it was neatly inscribed on the flyleaf: *Cecile Paté.*

Timushka was already ensconced at the far end of the salon, in one of its magnificent red chairs. Hilda perched on a smaller chair, like a prompter at Madame's ear. Journalists were expected—and photographers. Their names were typed on a list that rested on Hilda's lap.

Having ordered my invariable Virgin Mary from a young man

in black, my eye was caught by an arresting figure standing in the entrance from the lobby. He wore a plain dark suit with a Burberry draped across his shoulders. It was his hair that had commanded my attention—blond and shining, and a surprising contrast to his heavily lined face. I could see that he wore a boutonnière and carried a cane. His blue eyes scanned the room, as if he expected someone to come and kiss his hand.

Timushka noticed my interest and squinted in order to see him. She raised her glasses, worn on a velvet ribbon around her neck.

As the man entered the salon, it became clear at once that his walking-stick was no mere affectation. He needed it—and most profoundly. *Arthritis*, I thought. It was painful to watch his progress.

Timushka was glued to his every move. When it looked as if he was about to sit with his back to us, she laughed, and called out: "my dear! You almost had me believing I was invisible!"

At once, he turned and—beaming recognition and affection—he made straight for us.

"My dear one!"

"My darling!"

"You scamp!"

"You scallywag!"

He leaned down and kissed Timushka's cheeks and took her hands and kissed each one of them, his cane suspended like a pendulum, swinging between them. When the kissing was finished, he threw the Burberry from his shoulders into a chair and stepped behind Timushka to greet the Mouse.

"Hilda! Hilda! Hiding, as ever."

"Monsieur."

I noted that Hilda was blushing—with pleasure, I surmised. It was the first time I had seen her smile.

Timushka turned to me and said: "Miss Van Horne, may I present a very old friend, Erik Kelgard."

He bowed, or rather bobbed in my direction.

"Please. Be seated," said Timushka. "We are waiting for some journalists—but do have at least one drink with us."

He sat.

Erik Kelgard. His name meant nothing to me.

Timushka said: "before the war, we met in Denmark. I fell in love with him on sight."

"Now, now, Rose—none of that."

"But I did. I did. The most beautiful young man I had ever seen. And he danced like an angel."

Erik Kelgard looked at me and winked. "Pay no attention," he said.

"We had a love affair, Erik. Don't deny it."

"No. I will not deny it."

"All too brief—and then the war."

"All too brief—and then the war," he repeated.

"But after the war, we met again."

"Indeed. We met again."

"And I proposed." Timushka was smiling.

"Yes. You did."

"I proposed that Erik join my company and appear on stage with me. If Blackstone flourished a stunning blonde assistant, then I would do the same. But my blond would be a man."

Kelgard nodded.

"Oh, what heaven it was! Our heyday here in Paris. It was at the Marigny, was it not, that we perfected and performed the *Dancing Man* illusion for the very first time."

"Indeed."

"I saw it," I told them. "In New York and Boston. It was dazzling. To cut off his legs and then to restore them—all in plain sight. It was breathtaking ..."

"Yes. Just so. And the secret of it is at last to be revealed—in my book."

Erik Kelgard seemed amazed, and when he spoke, there was a touch of anger. "I thought," he said," that secret was to go to the grave with us."

"No," said Timushka. "Its revelation will cause a sensation, and I want to be around to enjoy it."

Kelgard shrugged. "You should have asked my permission," he said. "But—as you wish, my dear. And now, if you will excuse me ..." He beckoned to the waiter. "I should like the last round of drinks to go on my bill."

"No, no, Erik—you mustn't."

"Yes, yes. I must." He was firm. All at once, he seemed exhausted. "Let it be my gesture of greeting. I knew you were coming to Paris, Rose—and I was determined to be here. It may well be the last time we see each other."

"Oh, please—you mustn't say that."

"It is not I that says it. It is Time, my dear. We are both getting on. The clock is ticking."

"By the way," I said, in the hope of changing the subject—age can be so demeaning to old friends—"one of the chamber maids is a collector of autographs. I hope you don't mind, Madame Timushka, but I promised her yours."

"Of course."

I took the sketch-book from my bag and laid it on the table, opening it at the clean page following Molyneux's signature. Timushka tapped Hilda's knee and the Mouse produced a fountain pen. As the autograph was being elaborately produced, the waiter returned with the bill for Erik Kelgard. I watched him sign and, when Timushka had completed her task, I held out the book to him. "Would you?" I said. "I'm sure the young woman would be thrilled. She has already mentioned *The Dancing Man*."

"Forgive me, but declining autographs is a matter of principle. In the world of illusion in which I made my name—such as it was—it is best to keep the illusion intact." He struggled to his feet, employing the walking-stick, and I was certain that he was in pain. He retrieved his Burberry and blew a kiss at Timushka. "I shall rest now," he said, "and perhaps this evening, we shall dine."

"Of course we shall. Rest well, dear friend."

Erik Kelgard bowed—a trifle stiffly—and departed through the lobby to the elevators.

No sooner had he gone than Timushka said: "he's grown very old. But I like a face that tells the story of its life—don't you? That is why I never succumbed to the temptation of plastic surgery. *Timushka is as Timushka seems.* You may read it here." She gestured to her eyes—her mouth—her sunken cheeks. She did not, however, signify her flaming hair.

One of the journalists, with her photographer in tow, had appeared in the lobby and I could see her being directed to the salon.

"I think your inquisitors have begun to arrive," I said, and stood. "This has been delightful. I do hope I will see you again."

"You will, indeed," said Timushka. "We have not discussed your famous gardens."

"Perhaps tomorrow."

"Lunch. In the Brasserie here. Memory tells me the menu is superb."

"Twelve o'clock?"

"Make it one. Goodbye, my dear."

I said goodbye to Hilda and took my leave. Seconds later, I was back: "the autograph book."

"Of course."

On my way to the elevator, I decided not to tell Cecile Paté that I had failed to acquire the autograph of the man her mother had seen performing with Timushka. She would be too disappointed. Still—she had Timushka.

I unpacked my bags and lay down to rest. Jet-lag was catching up to me. At five o'clock, I was due to take a pill. It was now three-fifteen. No sooner, it seemed, had I drifted off than my telephone rang. It was ten past four. I had slept for almost an hour.

"Yes?" I was groggy.

"Miss Van Horne?"

"Indeed."

The voice was hushed and anonymous—I didn't recognize it at all.

"Would you come to Room 302. I beg of you."

"Who is this?"

"Hilda Menzies. Please. Please. It is urgent."

"Yes," I said. "I will come at once."

The Mouse hung up.

What can be wrong? I thought. She had sounded terrified.

My hair was a disaster, my face looked slept in—but I put myself together as quickly as I could. Before I left the room, I took my five-o'clock pill. No telling when I would return.

Room 302 was silent as I approached the door. When I knocked, there was an extended pause. Then Hilda said: "who is there?"

"Vanessa Van Horne."

I heard the lock turn over and saw Hilda's face. She was pale as a bar of Ivory soap. As she let me in, she raised her finger to her lips. I said nothing.

Number 302 was a suite and we were in the sitting-room. To the right, there was an open door.

From a distance, I heard Timushka's voice. "Is that Miss Van Horne?"

"Yes, Madame."

"I will come out."

Hilda drew me back and we waited. When Timushka appeared, she no longer wore her red wig. She was almost bald. What hair there was, was white. She now looked entirely her age—and shaken.

She closed the bedroom door and said: "please sit."

I did—and she did also.

"Some vodka, Hilda."

Hilda crossed the room and busied herself with bottles and glasses.

"What on earth has happened?" I asked.

"Erik Kelgard," she said.

"What about him?"

"He is in there." She pointed. "Dead."

"Dear God."

Hilda handed Timushka her vodka and turned to me. "Miss Van Horne?"

"Yes. But whisky." Thank heaven I had taken my pill. I could feel my heart racing.

"Dead? But how? And why in there?"

"He has committed suicide."

"Please?"

"He has committed suicide."

"By what means?"

"Strangulation. There is a silken cord around his throat. He has hanged himself. In the bathroom."

She drank—in fact, she gulped her vodka and held the glass out to Hilda. Hilda brought the bottle and gave her more.

"But we just saw him ..."

"Barely two hours ago at the very most. I simply can't think. I'm completely disoriented. Oh, Miss Van Horne! *Erik Kelgard.*"

She placed one fisted hand against her lips. "Why has he done this?"

"And why in there?" I looked at the bedroom door. "Did you find him?"

"Hilda found him. I was in here. My interviews were over and I had come up—like Erik—to have a rest. And then Hilda said: *you had best come and look, Madame.* And I went to the door ... and ..." Suddenly she turned on Hilda and hissed: "you should have warned me! Why didn't you warn me? Walking in there and seeing him that way—I nearly died. I sank to my knees. I could not believe it."

Hilda returned the vodka bottle to its place and sat down. I noted there was a handkerchief in her left hand. She had been weeping—but now was grimly silent.

I waited for a moment and then said: "have you called the hotel management?"

"No." Timushka was grim. "No. And I don't intend to. Not yet. I want a moment. I need a moment. I require a moment—just a moment, to take it in. To try to understand."

"Yes. Yes, of course." I waited. And then: "may I see him?" I said.

She hesitated. I wondered why. At last, she spoke—almost shyly.

"Yes," she said. "Please. That is why I called you. You seem so sensible. So practical. And I ..."

"It's all right," I told her. "I've dealt with worse than this." From 1942 to 1945 I had been imprisoned by the Japanese on the island of Java. Nothing since has matched what I witnessed there. "Do you want me to go in alone?"

"No. No. I will go in with you. But ..."

"Yes?"

Timushka looked at Hilda.

"I feel so helpless," she said. "Before you see him, there is something I must tell you."

I sat down again.

Timushka said: "that trick—*The Dancing Man?*"

"Yes. I remember."

"I must tell you how it was done."

"But why? And why now?"

She looked out the window and, when she spoke again, she went on watching the sky. Her voice was heavy and sad.

"You will recall that, right before your eyes, I cut off Erik's legs with a saw ..."

"Of course. It was astonishing."

"Most magicians—most illusionists perform such a trick by placing the so-called victim in an elaborate box—and when the cutting is done, the box is parted—giving the illusion the victim had been cut in half."

"Yes. But what made your illusion unique was the fact that we *saw* you cut through Erik Kelgard's legs—as you say, right before our very eyes. No box—no fancy draperies—you simply cut his legs off. Or gave that impression. And moments later ..."

"He rose, full-bodied, and we danced."

"You waltzed. It was delightful. And no one was ever able to tell how it was done. One minute he had no legs—and the next, he was dancing."

"The fact is—the fact was, Miss Van Horne, Erik Kelgard had no legs."

I was speechless. And then I thought: *of course. The way he walked. It wasn't arthritis, at all.*

"He lost them in an incident during the war. Both of them—below the knee." She waited for a moment and then continued. "What no one knew was that Erik had a twin brother. Absolutely identical." She looked at me and shrugged. "Oldest trick in the book," she said. "Not one man—but two. So that when I applied the saw, I was merely removing his false legs. They dropped, you may remember, into a basket. There was then a blinding flash of light—in which it seemed I restored his legs."

"Indeed."

"Whereas ... oh, dear—it is painful to remember. What actually happened was that the table on which Erik lay was flipped—and lying, secured to the underside, was Erik's twin. Edvard. All very simple. Edvard would rise and he and I would dance offstage while Erik would escape through a trap door."

"That's why the table was so thick. I do remember that. I used to think his legs were somehow doubled under him."

"No." She stood up. "I had to tell you this, because the man in there is legless ... Erik, for some mad reason, throwing his deformity in my face."

We crossed the room. Timushka opened the door.

The bedroom was much like my own—the same curtains, the same coverlet, the same chairs. On the bed, a man's dark suit was neatly folded. Beside it, also folded, a shirt and tie. On top of the jacket of the suit there was an envelope—and resting on the envelope, a wrist watch, a ring and a pair of spectacles.

I handed the note to Timushka and waited for her to read it.

Someone told me, once—a psychiatrist, I believe—that often, when people intend to kill themselves, they remove their watches and personal jewellery. Also their spectacles. Something about *finality*, I remember his saying. Something about *the moment of death*—an acknowledgement that all is over. No more use for adornment—no more references to time. And nothing more to see.

Timushka, having read, sat down. She held the letter out towards me. "I can't even finish it," she said. "It is all too sad."

I went to the window, where the light was better. The script was fastidious. Neat and carefully composed—written in black ink.

My dear Rose-Marie,

Do not be sorry for what I have done. It has been in my mind for the last six months and my only debate was how to do this—never whether I would or not. The pain of my injuries has begun to overwhelm me and I knew that my only fate could be to end up in some dreadful clinic, help-less and sedated, useless and alone. The thought of this was unbearable—and thus—my death.

I waited only to see you. That was right and that was good. I wish you well. I say to you: goodbye.

It was signed: *Your old friend and partner, Erik Kelgard.*

I folded it and set it beside his clothes. Then I went in and saw him where he was. What I found was the body of an old man with dyed blond hair. Death had done its usual work and had erased any sense of individuality from the face. A twisted silken cord, perhaps from a bathrobe, had been used. He was suspended from an iron bar that ran above the bath—a water or a wastage pipe. The body's state of undress revealed the double amputation—from the knees down. Both artificial legs—their harnesses undone—lay on the bottom of the tub. Erik Kelgard must have loosened their fastenings before attaching the cord to the pipe and then kicked the legs free—causing the cord to strangle him.

"We should telephone the management," I said, returning to the bedroom, "and they must call the police."

"Oh, no—no. Not the police."

"There will be no problem," I assured her. "The manager will be discreet. After all, it is in his own best interests. The police will understand that, too. More than likely, they will simply say that Mister Kelgard had a heart attack."

I placed the phone call, saying only that we required a doctor in Room 302 and that perhaps the manager himself should accompany him. I did not explain and the secretary at the other end asked no questions.

When they arrived, the doctor turned out to be a woman—le docteur Mercredi—*Doctor Wednesday.* She was middle-aged, obliging and absolutely professional. I liked and trusted her at once. The manager—Monsieur Lemaître—was equally reassuring. Gentle, understanding and not the least obsequious. As I told them what had happened and while Timushka explained who Erik Kelgard was and how long she had known him, they listened to us with an air of sympathy. Nothing of what a person might expect if all this had happened in New York. *Was this man your lover? Do you really expect us to believe you have no idea why he killed himself in* your *bathroom?*

A matronly woman, whom I think is in charge of the cleaning staff, was called in to help move Timushka to another equally charming suite on my floor. *You will, of course, no longer be comfortable in these rooms* is what the manager said. What I think he really meant was: *as soon as you have been moved, we will call the police and let them inspect the location of Kelgard's death and remove the body.*

For the first time, I had a twinge of uncertainty about the word *suicide* concerning what had happened. This was when I explained to the manager that the clothes on the bed were those of the dead man. His shirt—his tie—his trousers—his jacket ... but, strangely ...

Where was the Burberry? And where the walking-stick?

And where was the boutonnière?

Of course, he would have gone to his own room after leaving us. His luggage would be there. But—since his condition had so obviously put him in an increasing amount of pain, why—and *how*—had he come to Timushka's suite without the walking-stick?

The Burberry one could understand. Anyone would shed his overcoat. But the walking-stick—the boutonnière?

Stranger and stranger.

I consented to wait with Timushka in her new suite of rooms because she seemed to be reassured by my company. The police, we knew, would want to question us once they had done their preliminary inspection. I had been correct, it turns out, in saying the hotel would explain the incident as the result of "an unfortunate heart attack." I was told so this evening, returning from dinner.

Hilda Menzies was also being moved to the fourth floor because it was absolutely essential to Madame's state of mind and health that her secretary-companion be right next door. This caused something of a furore, since the room next to the suite now occupied by Timushka already had an occupant. And he was not at all happy when asked to move.

Hilda was still downstairs repacking when all this took place. Timushka, who had redonned her wig, was sitting in the new suite drinking vodka. The manager, Lemaître, was next door trying to placate the angry patron—whose voice we could hear through the wall.

"Oh, do go and see what they're on about," Timushka said. "Surely they don't need to scream and yell."

I went into the corridor.

There was, of course, no "screaming and yelling," but the Angry Patron was doing the next best thing.

The door was open and I could see M. Lemaître's back. He did not raise his voice. He was telling the man that "a perfectly beautiful room awaited him" and also that he would not be charged for his stay at the Lutétia. I must admit, these are terms I would have accepted, but they did not satisfy the Angry Patron.

"Who the hell is Timushka, to tell me what to do?"

I tried my best to see him, but he thwarted me by remaining behind the opened door.

Poor, dear Hilda then appeared with her belongings and a bell-hop. She looked like a refugee—both her person and her luggage in disarray.

On hearing Angry's voice, she stopped in her tracks. "This should not be happening," she said. "Can you make them stop?"

No.

Angry was adamant. Hilda listened to his voice with—it occurred to me—an astonished expression that did not match the weight of what was being said.

At last, the manager gave up the fight. Angry would not be moved—no matter what—and the only answer was to capitulate. Such arguments can only be driven so far before they begin to endanger a hotel's reputation.

Before the door to Angry's now undisputed territory was closed, I finally caught a glimpse of him—a very old man, bald, toothless—and enraged. There was also something that both startled and intrigued me. More than likely, just a coincidence—but still of interest. Draped on the back of a chair, a Burberry coat of the very same colour as the one I had seen worn by Erik Kelgard.

Of course, there must be at least two hundred such coats in Paris—but given the context, I could not help thinking how odd it was—what with the last one I had seen belonging to a man now dead, and his oldest friend just taking up residence in the rooms next door. To say nothing of his acquaintance standing by my side.

As it turned out, there was a patron directly across the hall from Timushka's suite who was not at all troubled when asked to move. And delighted to be told there would be no charge for her stay.

We took Hilda's things into the suite, while the change was effected, and half an hour later she was ensconced.

I was still haunted by the face of the Angry Patron. It was trying to remind me of something—or of someone.

When the police came, there were two of them—an inspector, M. Monet, and a sergeant in uniform, whose name we were not told. M. Lemaître and Doctor Mercredi were also present. M. Lemaître went back to his office once M. Monet started asking questions.

The first thing he wanted to know was when we had last seen Erik Kelgard. Sometime between 14:45 and 15:00 hours.

Monet turned to Doctor Mercredi. "So he died soon after that," he said.

Doctor Mercredi replied: "I would say between 15:00 and 16:00 hours."

"And does he have any family?"

"He had one brother—but, far as I know, he never married."

I had a thought.

"Where is the brother? What did you say his name is?"

"Edvard." This was Hilda.

"And do you know where he is?"

"Dead. For many years. Ten, at least."

Oh.

Hilda interlaced her fingers and started folding her handkerchief.

Inspector Monet wanted an explanation. "His brother?" he asked.

Timushka explained that Erik and Edvard were twins.

"Identical twins?"

"Absolutely. Except that each was the mirror image of the other. One was right-handed and one left-handed."

I had noted in the salon that Erik had signed the bill with his left hand. And also, the left-hand slant to the writing in the suicide note.

Timushka continued: "and then, of course, the most obvious difference was the fact that, tragically, Erik had lost his legs."

"And when did that happen?"

"During the war. In Denmark. Erik was in the Resistance. They were setting some sort of explosive device in place when it blew up. An accident. And he lost his legs."

"I see. And the brother—Edvard, you say?"

"Yes."

"When did you last see him?" Monet asked.

Hilda coughed.

"Twelve years ago," Timushka said. "On what turned out to be my farewell tour. I was only sixty-eight. I did not intend to retire until, like Dietrich, I was seventy. I had said: *if Marlene can still produce her magic at that age, so can I.* But then ..." She drank more vodka. "It was such a terrible time. The memory of it is unkind—and I try not to dwell on it."

She explained *The Dancing Man* illusion to Inspector Monet and Doctor Mercredi. Then she said:

"Edvard had grown tired of it. More than tired. Sick. When we travelled, because of the secrecy surrounding how the illusion was created, Edvard always had to wear a disguise. He was never able to be himself."

"Never," said Hilda.

"Of course, on occasion, he would break loose and we would lose him for a day or two. Three days at the most. We were his only means of support, you see. He could not live without us. But his ill temper was dreadful. He started arguing with me, calling me a *slave-driver*—claiming that I'd ruined his life by denying him his own identity. Then he would turn on Erik. It was awful. Finally, he disappeared. We were on tour in Australia—and had just arrived in Perth."

Hilda smiled and looked away. *Perth,* she seemed to say.

"As you may know, Perth is on the southeastern tip of Australia. A world unto itself. It was there that we saw the last of Edvard. He stood, one day, in the Indian Ocean—hurling stones and epithets at us. At me, at Erik, at Hilda ..."

Yes.

"There was such a crowd on the beach, that day—and when a group of young people ran between us, we lost sight of him entirely. By the time the group had passed, Edvard had disappeared—and we never saw him again."

There was a sigh—perhaps from Doctor Mercredi, perhaps from Hilda—and this was followed by a profound silence.

At last, Inspector Monet rose and said: "Madame, you have my sympathy. An autopsy will be performed this evening. In the morning, we may have an answer. In the meantime, I urge you to mourn your friend and think no more of the circumstance in which he died. If the question has an answer, we shall find it. If there is none—then none should be sought. Erik Kelgard is dead. An episode has ended. Let us seek reason—but above all, let us seek reconciliation. Reality is what we have to live with. Let us live."

I thought: *my goodness, what a wonderful thing to say. And in such a difficult moment.* My respect for the French police rose, in the aftermath, one hundred per cent.

Back in my room, I began to feel relief that the whole dreadful incident was drawing to a close. Still, I was nagged by one or two images. The Burberry in the room of the Angry Patron—and the elusive familiarity of his face—and the reaction, incident by incident, of Hilda Menzies.

Suddenly, I had a thought and went immediately to the telephone. I asked to be connected with Madame Timushka's new suite.

It was the Mouse who answered—Hilda Menzies. She said that

Madame was resting, but I persuaded Hilda to go in and put a single question to her. When the answer was finally delivered, it confirmed the notion that had been growing in my mind. Clearly, something must be done.

Reluctant to go to the police with my suspicions, I decided to pursue the matter on my own.

There was no answer when, a few minutes later, I knocked on the door of the Angry Patron's room. This was no surprise, but I was determined to gain entrance. And if I was in luck, there was a relatively simple way of doing it.

Luck was, indeed, with me. After looking in through each open door on the fourth floor, I located Cecile Paté tidying up one of the vacated rooms. She was still effusively grateful for the Timushka autograph I had added to her collection, and after only a little persuasion, she agreed to let me into the room I was so eager to see. I said that it was an emergency, and that I had arranged to meet the police there—which, given my intentions to call them, was only a slight deviation from the truth.

Once the door had been opened, I said to her: "you must leave, now. I know what I must do—and all will be well."

Poor Cecile. She wasn't certain that what she was doing was proper. I tried to reassure her—and off she went.

Once she had left, I thought it wisest to lock the door. Knowing that, in doing so, I was placing myself—to whatever degree—in jeopardy, I knew I had to accept the risk.

"Where are you?" I said. "I know you are here."

There was not a sound.

"Mister Kelgard, I am not the police. I am an American in France on holiday. My name is Vanessa Van Horne. Madame Timushka has become an acquaintance—all by pure chance. It is only through her that I know anything at all of who you are and what might have happened to your brother. Please believe me: I am the only one who suspects you may have witnessed his death. And, if that is true, then you are the only one who can solve this mystery."

Still, not a sound.

I was beginning to think I was wasting my breath on an empty room.

I went to the closet and opened the door.

The geography of this room was sufficiently akin to my own that I knew where the light switch was. Of course—and wouldn't you know it—the bulb had burned out. Burned out, or had been twisted so as not to function.

Reaching, I inadvertently knocked some object to the floor. Perhaps an umbrella. I stooped and found it. Not an umbrella. A walking-stick.

The walking-stick. Eric Kelgard's, last seen in the salon. I recognized it instantly. There was the butterfly handle I had noted as the walking-stick was propped against the edge of Eric's chair.

I went into the bathroom, stick in hand. No one. Returning to the bedroom, I inspected the curtains. Still, no one. And yet, he must be in the room. But where?

Under the bed? I lifted its skirts with the stick. Still and ever—no one.

I sat down.

"Where are you?"

I said this aloud, but really only to myself.

If not in the closet, then in the bathroom. If not in the bathroom, then behind the curtains. If not behind the curtains, then ...

Under the bed.

As in *The Dancing Man.*

I am not as supple as I once was. The me that used to stride through Central Park once a day and who got down on her hands and knees, creating rockeries and planting trees, is gone. Still, it must be done. I was certain I knew where the Angry Patron was and how he had managed to stay there, silent for so long.

And I was right.

Dropping to a kneeling position, I slowly lowered myself until I was prone. Lifting the skirts of the bed, I saw that he was there, exactly as I had imagined—and precisely as once he had clung to the underside of the "table" on which his brother had lain to have his legs removed.

"That's quite a trick, Mister Kelgard," I said. "Come out at once."

I was tempted to add that Holmesian phrase which always made me smile: *the game is up!* But I refrained—and, using the walking-stick, pulled and pushed myself to my feet.

Seconds later, but on the other side of the bed, Edvard Kelgard appeared.

Without his blond wig, he seemed very old. But it was certainly the face of the man I had met in the salon. The man who had pretended to be his twin brother, Erik.

He said nothing.

I sat down.

Slowly, he came around the bed, went to the bureau and removed a bottle of whisky. He went with this to a table where glasses stood with an ice-bucket on a tray.

At last, he spoke.

"Will you?" he said.

"Indeed." And would be very glad of it. Two glasses of whisky in one day! Vanessa Van Horne, take care.

But I didn't care. For the moment, I was exhilarated and feeling quite young.

Once he had handed me the glass, he sat in the chair across from me and lighted a cigarette. He was in his shirt sleeves and had removed his tie in order to leave it with the rest of Erik's clothes on Timushka's bed.

He sipped at his drink, refusing to look me in the eye. "How did you know I was here?" he asked.

"Blind chance," I told him. "My luck—and your misfortune. If you thought about it, you might guess—but I won't leave you dangling. The fact is, it took me longer to twig than it should have. Timushka has just confirmed that it was Erik Kelgard who was the right-handed twin. Since, when I saw you signing your bill, I noted the use of your left hand, I realized it had not been Erik I had met—but Edvard. And besides—there was Hilda ..."

I paused to let Edvard take all this in—but the pause was not required. No sooner had I finished than he gave a great sigh and sat back in his chair.

"Hilda. Yes. She would know my voice was not his. We ..."

"You were once lovers."

He smiled. And shrugged, It was sad. They had been lovers—*yes*—but so what? As always, the woman had been loyal—the man not.

Do I mean *as always?* Perhaps not. My father loved my mother and died for it. All those years ago. In Java. He escaped his prison and made for help—and was shot. And Edvard Kelgard was not a man to break free and die. On the contrary: he had broken free and run away.

"Of course, you realized my little performance with the walking-stick and the limp was just that—a performance."

I nodded.

"Also, that I must have written Erik's suicide note." He mimed the act of writing with his left hand. "Yes?"

"Yes."

I looked away. At first, I had realized no such thing. I had noticed the slant of the writing on the note, but had simply presumed Erik Kelgard had been the left-handed twin.

Edvard went on. "I am so accustomed to the sight of my penmanship, I forget how distinctive and tell-tale it is." He sighed. "It was the one significant difference between us: his right-hand-edness and my *gaucherie*, as our charming mother used to say. Our charmingly vicious—charmingly mean-spirited mother. I was never allowed to forget it. At school, they even tried to beat it out of me. But I was incapable of changing. Utterly helpless ..."

He smiled and stubbed out his cigarette. "It proved to be something of a problem for Timushka, too. You see—*I* was the *Dancing Man* and she could not abide being led from the left as we waltzed off-stage."

"You killed him. But, why?"

"I killed him because he had ruined my life. Ruined it. Destroyed it, utterly."

"That doesn't sound likely, Mister Kelgard, from what I've heard of your brother."

"No. I know. He was always so well thought of. And the truth is, I had ruined his life long before he ruined mine." I waited.

Edvard got up and poured more whisky into his glass. I declined.

"It was because of me that Erik lost his legs."

"I don't understand. It was in the war—an accident of some kind."

"That's true. Quite true. But the accident would not have occurred if ..."

"Yes?"

He was evidently in some despair regarding what he must say. It was clearly painful for him—but he did, at last, manage to continue.

"In Denmark, you may well be aware, there was not a great deal of resistance during the war. Hardly any, at first. But—in time—a movement grew ..." He waited again—and then went on. "I was not part of it. The Movement. But Erik was. And our charming mother goaded me ... into betraying him. She was a fascist, you see. A Nazi. Some of the aristocracy, a lot of the upper class—this happened everywhere in Europe, by the way, more than has ever been admitted—they used the presence of the Germans to gain their own ends."

"I was aware of some of that," I said. "But not a great deal."

"Erik was *in our way*, according to our mother. *Endangering our chances of survival. Think what would happen to us all—to your father, your sisters—and to me. And to you, if Erik was to persist in this madness.* To persist in this madness—called resistance. And I ... I gave in. I collapsed, you might say, under her tyranny."

"I'm so sorry. What a dreadful time it was."

"Yes. Yes. It was. Dreadful. And, because I told... because I *indicated* that a shipment of coal was going to be sabotaged—men from the S.S. were sent to prevent it."

He emptied his glass.

I watched him, not without sympathy. The confession of a crime is hard at best—but when it involves your own family, it must be doubly difficult to articulate.

"I told no names. Not even my own. I telephoned from a kiosk—gave the information—and went home. Erik disappeared for over half a year. When he returned, he had lost both his legs. I was sickened, of course. Devastated. And, when Mother died, two years after the war, I told him ... I told Erik what we had done. What I had done."

"That must have required a good deal of courage."

"No. Not courage. Relief. I had to tell, or I would have gone mad."

"And so ...?"

I hadn't realized, until he turned and I could see his face, that—for a moment—he had wept. Now, he wiped his eyes and blew his nose and poured himself another drink. At last, he said: "what was your question?"

"Why did you kill him?"

"*Why did I kill him?*" He shook his head. "In time—I came not just to fear him, but to hate him."

"Fear him?"

"Yes. He was blackmailing me. That was how, in the end, he kept me with him. He would tell the world what I had done, if I left him without his career. Because, if I left him, he would have no career. There could be no *Dancing Man* without the two of us. The Kelgard twins. In Australia, I left and went into hiding. I let them think I was dead. Even Hilda. But the truth is, it was only then that I learned how to live. How to be alive as myself. Myself and only myself. Me, and me only. For over ten years ... I was free. You've no idea what my life had been like. Everywhere we went, I had to go in disguise. No one must ever know there were two of us. And so, every night as we left the theatre, I got back into my make-up, while everybody else got out of theirs. I was known as Harald Köenig because of my accent. Well—there you have it. When Erik discovered I was still alive—having spent a fortune tracking me down with hired agents—I said: *enough is enough.* Having gained my freedom, I simply could not bear to give it up."

We sat long into the twilight and, as darkness fell, Edvard Kelgard moved about the room and turned on the lights. We might have been old companions, drinking whisky, telling tales. It was an odd sensation.

He finished by saying: "I knew that Timushka was coming to Paris, preparing to publish her memoirs. I wrote to Erik—who was in Copenhagen—suggesting that we *stage* our reconciliation here. A fairy-tale ending—everyone living happily ever after—basking in the beaming light of our fairy godmother's smile."

He became very matter of fact.

"I said we must be in the Lutétia when she arrived. He agreed. He came two days ago. I was waiting for him—here in this room. I had registered in his name. This afternoon, I was sure that Timushka would be holding forth to journalists for two hours or more. That would give me plenty of time. And the rest you have guessed. In the salon, I had the misfortune ...," he smiled, "... to meet the elegant Miss Van Horne. Having left your company, I came upstairs and, using techniques employed in the world of illusions, I got us into Timushka's suite. Erik thought we were going to surprise her there. He was so excited. Like a child. Still—I killed him. Hung his body in the bathroom—arranged his clothes and placed them with the note on the bed. Perfect—if it had not been for you."

"What do you intend to do about this, Mister Kelgard?"

He was standing.

He looked about him.

"I intend," he said, smiling, "to take a breath of air."

Having spoken, he turned towards the window farthest from where I was seated, lifted the sash and leapt to his death.

He fell four storeys down—and through the high glass ceiling of the salon where I had first made his acquaintance.

Telling Hilda will be hardest of all. Timushka will understand.

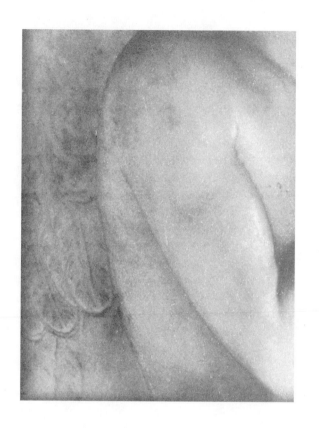

A Bag of Bones

1

TUESDAY—AND AS ALWAYS, Minna's disgruntled sighs could be heard throughout the house as she made her way from bedroom to bathroom, kitchen to dining-room. There, amidst the heirloom Georgian silver, the Spode, the Sheraton chairs and the Adams sideboards, she would stand before the table, heave the last of her sighs and nudge the French doors shut behind her, using her elbow while she lighted the first of the day's cigarettes. *Well,* she would say aloud, *let's go.*

The table, once her mother's pride and joy, could not be seen beneath the stacks of books and piles of paper, the bottles of Sheaffer's blue-black ink, the overflowing ashtrays, the coffee mugs with the mouldy remains of last week's brew—and the empty glasses, some of them Waterford, most of them Woolworth's. A captain's chair with broken spindles lay on its side where, rising from Friday's labours, Minna had tipped it. Now, it was Tuesday. Again.

I work a four-day week, Bragg. A four-day week. Don't fuck me around on this. I work a four-day week—that's all there is to it. No argument.

Stuart Bragg worked a five-day week at his desk upstairs. Meticulous. The hours were often crazy, but Monday to Friday, one way or another—all day or all night—he was up there, leaning forward into the light surrounding his hands, one hand poised with its pen above the page, the other flicking ashes from its cigarette. He never missed the ashtray. Never. And when his pen at last began to move, a sentence long considered would be inscribed without a second's hesitation. Bragg would then scan what he had written, put its period in place and re-cap the pen, for fear its ink might run dry before the next sentence was ready for the page.

Not Minna. Tuesdays to Fridays she became a storm centre, generating blizzards of paper, writing at furious speed, throwing the pages over her shoulder onto the floor. Only when the whole day's work was done would she rise and bend to pick them up by the handful. Then she would lay them out in unnumbered piles on the table, weighting each pile with a stone from the garden or a brick from the dumpster next door where a house was being destroyed. When all the piles were in place, Minna would give a conclusive sigh—the kind induced by a smile—and emerge for the day's first bottle of Côtes du Rhone. (Sometimes, the first acknowledged bottle.)

I work a four-day week, Bragg. You work a five. By Friday, you have two pages—I have fifty.

"If you can find them."

"Who cares if I can find them? They're there." Minna squinted at him through her smoke. "You may be able to find your pages, my dear—but can you find any words on them?" She snorted.

"That was uncalled for."

"*Every*thing is called for between you and me. Every god-damned everything you can think of. Jesus! You make me so damned mad. All that talent—talent other people would kill for, just to have one-tenth of it—and you won't even let it out to play. You're just like my god-damned mother." Minna drank and puffed. "She never let me leave the god-damned house for fear I'd be run down by a truck or raped. Or because she thought I'd be *misunderstood. Me*—that was crazy! Of course I'd be misunderstood! Holy God. Try being alive, Bragg. Open the door. Let your talent go free. If someone can't cope with it, that's their problem— not yours. NOT YOURS, my dear—my darling."

She smiled.

"*Not yours.*" She made a jabbing gesture at him, softening her voice. Then she stood up, leaned in over his chair and kissed him on the forehead. "I love you," she said. "I love you, Bragg."

"Yes," he said. "I can tell."

2

They lived in Toronto. Their house was on Collier Street and looked out over the ravine, down towards the Rosedale Valley Road. In winter, the children from the neighbourhood were taken there with sleds and toboggans and gently pushed down the hill and dragged back up by exhausted parents. But the parents didn't seem to mind. *Why else have children,* Minna had said, *if you aren't going to pull them uphill? If you're only going to watch them slide away from you down to the bottom, what good does that do anyone?*

Spring and summer, Stuart Bragg would sit at the top of the hill on a bench, with Ben, his dog, leaning in against his legs. Autumns, they would go together into the depths of the ravine, underneath the bridges, all the way to the valley of the Don. Along this route, Ben would rush up and down the wooded hillsides, chasing squirrels and, on occasion, rabbits—though the rabbits now were scarce. Ben never caught anything. He was an Irish terrier and rats had been the cause of his breeding. All the rats lived down along the dumpy edge of the river, where they survived on a diet of rotting bits and pieces of Harvey's hamburgers thrown down in paper bags from passing cars. That and McDonald's milk-shake cartons, chip-boxes, styrofoam cups. Farther south, down towards Dundas and Queen streets, the rats competed for these leavings with various human itinerants—alcoholics, bag ladies, street kids. Bragg and Ben never went down there. That was Minna's territory.

Most days, when Bragg had risen from his desk—all his sentences done and filed in the folder, each rewritten twenty times—he would put on whatever outdoor clothing the season demanded, whisper to Ben and leave the house. He never called to Ben indoors. The sound of human voices was the only thing Minna would not tolerate as she wrote. Falling walls, breaking glass, the machine-gun fire of pneumatic drills—all of which were in evidence next door—barely registered in Minna's ears. Music was acceptable—of any kind. Revving motorcycles, back-firing cars—she was deaf. But a human voice, if it spoke inside the house, was anathema.

Once on the sidewalk, Bragg and Ben would turn towards the park overlooking the ravine and some days descend and other days not. Just to be beneath the sky, and not beneath the ceiling, was a godsend. There was always a moment when man and dog would both look up at the blue beyond the trees and Bragg would smile and Ben would wag his tail.

"Great, eh?" said Bragg.

Yes, said Ben.

This day in April—not quite all the way to spring—they chose the bench and both of them sat there on its green painted planks. It was still too cold to sit on the cracked cement beneath the bench, so Ben jumped up and occupied the end away from Bragg.

Bragg had smoked all morning and all afternoon. Now, he decided not to. He wound his scarf a little looser over his chest and pulled the finger-ends of his gloves until they were not so tight. His father had taught him that. *Air is insulation. Sleeping naked, you're warmer in winter and cooler in summer than when you wear pyjamas ...*

Fathers are founts, Bragg thought. *Something I will never be. A fount. No one over whom I can flood my wisdom ...* Bragg smiled. For a moment. Then he didn't. He had thought to use the sentences just uncurled in his work. Then he thought of their deeper, their truer implication. *No children. Ever.*

None?

None. It is my decree. I have spoken.

"Never?"

He said the last aloud.

Ben looked up expectantly.

Bragg reached out and fondled the dog's ears.

It was then—just then—that he saw the boy at the foot of the hill. Boy. Man. Which?

Ben went back to dozing.

The sun had begun its slide towards evening. A robin sang. The boy—the man—the young man was wearing rugby shorts and a rugby shirt. Blues and greens. He had been running in the valley and had returned this far and stopped. Perhaps it was one of his first spring runs and perhaps he was out of condition—though he didn't look it. His thighs were squared with muscles. His torso filled the shirt.

Bragg squinted.

When was that—the last time lust had reached his groin? God. He could not remember.

He imagined the runner—who was seated now on the grass below him—going home and stripping off his clothes. Rugby shirt. Rugby shorts. Running shoes. Jock strap ... That was always the order in Bragg's mind—the running shoes and the jock strap last ... Then the figure gleaming in the shower, finally obscured by steam.

The lad stood up below him and brushed the seat of his shorts. Leaves. Damp and mouldy. *Oh ...*

Bragg closed his eyes.

Go away. When I open them again, be gone. There's an old man dying on the hill up here. You'll see him, if you turn around to look.

Bragg counted to a hundred. Surely, by now, he would have departed.

No. But nearly. The runner was moving away towards the corner, starting already to jog. He disappeared beyond the trees and the obtrusive shapes of passing cars. Bragg was glad he had not been able to see the final direction taken. He did not want to know where the runner lived. If the street was known, and the house was numbered, the boy would be able to close a real door, depriving Bragg of his sprinting ghost.

3

"They've found something," Minna said, as Bragg and Ben came through the door.

"They? Who?"

Ben went up the stairs to the landing and lay down.

"Next door. The wreckers."

Minna moved towards the kitchen. Bragg could tell she'd already been out there. In her hurry to consolidate her advantage, she had left the doors to the dining-room open and he could see a half-drunk bottle of wine anchoring some of her pages on the table.

"What?" said Bragg. "Found what?"

They had arrived on either side of the kitchen table, Minna turning back from the cupboard with two bottles of wine: her Côtes du Rhone (*my first today, Bragg*) and his Beaujolais. She let him draw the corks, affecting a kind of unnatural nonchalance that he knew was due to the fact she'd already started drinking twenty minutes ago.

"Glasses," he said.

She got them down and placed them on the table.

"So," he said, pouring. "What?"

"A baby," said Minna. "Bones. They were in the wall."

"Dear God," said Bragg. "Dear God in heaven." He shoved Minna's glass towards her and placed the Côtes du Rhone beside it. They never sat at the kitchen table—they always stood. There weren't any chairs. Somewhere, perhaps behind the cellar door, there was a stool. It was never used.

"They've taken them away, I think. Or the coroner has. Or someone. In a bag ..."

"Did they know how old they were?"

"I told you. A baby."

"No. I mean how long the bones had been there."

"Who knows? These were workers' houses first," said Minna, referring to all the houses on Collier Street. "Mid-nineteenth century, I guess. It wasn't gentrified here until after the First World War."

"Could they tell if the baby had been killed? Or did it just die?"

"Nothing *just dies*, Bragg. There's always a reason." Minna looked at her hands. "They think it must have been murdered."

"People don't murder babies."

"Oh? Gee. I hadn't realized ..." Minna smiled and sucked on her cigarette—then on her wine. "Not even Einstein—not even Alfred North Whitehead could have conjured the number of murdered babies, Bragg. People do it all the time. Especially women."

"I can't believe that."

"Believe it. It's the truth."

They stood there.

Ben came out of the darkened hall and sat in the doorway.

Bragg looked at him. "Baby dogs ...," he said. "That I would understand. Baby cats. Always unwanted."

"We're talking human babies here, Bragg. Please don't sentimentalize this. It's deadly serious—you should pardon the fucking pun ..."

Bragg now realized Minna was weeping. She had turned away from him, ostensibly to find another cigarette. Now, she turned back.

"Why are you crying?" he asked her, gently as he could—the way he might have whispered to Ben. "Because of Alma?" Alma was Minna's sister. Had been.

"Alma wasn't a baby. She was eleven. Sure as fate, my parents killed her."

Bragg had heard all this before. *I can feel it here,* Alma would say. *It hurts,* she'd told Minna. Screaming. *Right side—the abdomen.* But the parents did not believe in doctors. They had insisted it was only something Alma had eaten. And she had died. Of a burst appendix. Shrieking.

Bragg closed his eyes. He knew that Alma's death—the reason for it and the manner—was one of Minna's nightmare burdens. The mother who wouldn't let Minna leave the house had also locked out the doctors, who might have saved Alma. Eleven. When Minna was nine. And now, this child next door, a bag of bones. "I'm sorry," he said. As if he needed to apologize for everyone else's sins.

"Thing is," said Minna, "most women want their babies, want them to live. Survive. But all these others ... I can't imagine not wanting a life," she said. "I simply can't imagine it. I don't mean abortion. Abortions are sometimes necessary. Kate's, for instance. Rosemary's ..." Friends whose lives had been saved. "But these— this other. How can it happen?"

Bragg said nothing.

"Still, I know it does happen," Minna said. "I've seen it with my own eyes. Babies found in garbage cans down around Queen Street. Wrapped up in towels inside of green plastic bags. In garbage cans and dumpsters. Out behind restaurants. Out behind factories. Out behind houses. Jesus."

There was not a trace of vehemence in her voice. Only amazement. *Jesus.*

Then she laughed.

Bragg had been rolling the ash from the end of his cigarette. Now, he looked up. Minna's laughter seemed to be genuine—humorous—not ironic. "Yes?" He smiled expectantly—pleased that she had recovered her poise.

"I just had this image of the woman next door. 1910—1928. Whenever. I just had this image of her standing in the living-room, waiting for her father, waiting for her husband—maybe her mother—someone who'd been away a long, long time and was just returning. *Oh, hello, my dear*—whoever. *Hello, my dear, my darling. Guess what I've been doing while you were gone?* Who would have guessed it? Who *could* have guessed? *I've been repapering the bedroom!* The bathroom. The living-room. Upstairs, downstairs and in my lady's chamber ... Jesus. Jesus. Jesus Christ. UPSTAIRS—DOWNSTAIRS—AND IN MY LADY'S CHAMBER! BURYING BABIES!"

Bragg stood frozen.

Minna's laughter was silenced—stopped abruptly as if a door had slammed on it.

"Bones in a bag," she said. "A bag of bones I would have killed for."

4

Upstairs in the bathroom, sometime after midnight, Bragg stood looking into the mirror. Where had he gone?

The man staring back at him appeared to be a stranger. He gave a smile that Bragg had never seen before. *Have we met?* he said. *If we have, I don't recall the name ...*

Bragg ran the taps. He felt cold. He wanted noise. He put the plug in place and let the basin fill up with water. Hot. All but scalding. Raising his eyes, he gave the stranger a sideways look— almost shyly.

"My name is Stuart Bragg," he said.

Had he spoken aloud?

Yes.

He pulled the plug in order to create more noise, all the water plunging down the drain with a shout. Then he put the plug back in and, while the basin refilled, he began to hum. Nothing of music, only a kind of *uhm*—an *ohm*—extended, wavering above the flow. If Minna could hear him, she would think it was just *Bragg's aria*, always off-key. *Even deaf people sing when they turn on the taps ...*

Bragg placed his hands in the water. And instantly withdrew them. Parboiled.

Don't. Say nothing. Close your eyes and count to ten. Count to twenty. Thirty. Sixty.

There.

Cooked hands. Oh, God.

He elbowed the cold water tap and put his fingers into its stream. He would think of something else. Anything.

There's an old man dying on the hill.

Where had he heard that? Someone had said it.

You said it.

When?

This afternoon, sitting on the bench with Ben, when that boy ...

I don't like boys.

Boy. Man. Whatever. Certainly he was male.

And his legs ...

And his legs?

Don't.

Rugby shorts. Rugby shirt. Running shoes. Jock strap. Eh, Bragg?

Stop that.

Look at me.

Bragg looked into the mirror.

How old am I?

Ninety.

How old are you?

Thirty-five.

Go and get yourself a runner, Bragg. Go and get yourself a naked runner.

Bragg's hands went numb. Or practically. The water coming from the tap was frigid. *Icelandic*, Minna would have called it.

Speak of the devil. She was standing in the doorway.

"Aren't you coming to bed?"

"No."

"Don't be ridiculous. Stop driving up the water bill and get some sleep."

"I'm going to do some writing."

"All right. Go ahead. Do some writing. I'm away, now. Outa here."

"'Night."

"Good night."

She was gone. He shut the door. It had been a close call. She had almost caught him with an erection.

5

Minna's publisher was a woman whose name was Kate Dance. She was one of the very few people who, in Minna's eyes, could do no wrong. Bragg did not care for her, but that was beside the point. More importantly, Kate did not care for Bragg. She thought he was bad for Minna—that he acted as a restraint—a handicap—holding Minna back because she was always so concerned about his "problems."

Kate acknowledged that Bragg was talented. *Very*, she said. Which was true. *But the talented have to learn to take care of themselves.* She smiled pointedly at Minna. *Themselves, not others. Others are a drag on talent. And significant others weigh a ton.*

"I wouldn't rid myself of him if you paid me a million dollars," Minna said.

"You'd probably have a million dollars, if it wasn't for Bragg."

"Bragg my *impedimenta*? Bull shit."

That was the end of it. Except at home on Collier Street. There, Minna joked about it. *You're my Bragg-and-baggage,* she would say. *I have to lug you everywhere I go.* She called him *Mister Millstone* and *Mister Albatross* and *Mister Inhibition.* Finally, he told her to stop.

"It's beginning to sound as if you believe it."

"I don't believe a word of it, Bragg. Not to worry. I love you. I love you and I'm going to have your babies." She smiled after saying this, and raised her glass. "We'll call them *Shack* and *Fett.* Short for *Shackle* and *Fetter.*" This made her roar.

Bragg was glad of the laughter. It put an end to the topic of children. His fear of them could not be communicated. It was not unlike having an illness which, as yet, had acquired no name— and for which there was no cure.

They had discussed it—argued about it—worried it to death—shouted about it—screamed. Bragg was serious—not neurotic about it, even though Minna accused him of this from time to time. *Why?* she would whisper. *Why?* she would bellow. *Why?* she would tease.

Why?

Because he was homosexual.

Because ... in the past, members of his family had been born with genetic defects. Club feet—cleft palates—schizophrenia— Down's Syndrome. Jesus. Enough was enough.

"To say nothing of the fact," he had said to Minna one day, "I'm probably a genetic homosexual."

"There's no such thing, Bragg."

"How do we know? The question is still out there."

"A *genetic* homosexual? Come off it."

"If you're born this way—and I was—then where the hell else did it come from? My genes are telling me: *don't.* No more babies. No more babies. This is the end of the line."

"Bull shit."

That, for a while, was the last of it.

Bragg always wore a condom—*just in case.* He claimed it was because of AIDS, in spite of the fact that, secretly, he'd gone for blood tests and knew he was HIV negative. Minna hated the condoms and said so. *Every time we're ready to go, you have to stop and put on a stupid fucking rubber.*

Bragg began to hide them. What if she stuck them with pins and the sperm got through? What if she stole them? What if she cut them up with scissors? The Lorena Bobbit of the condom world.

He hid them in his desk drawer, layered amongst the boxes of ink cartridges. He hid them in the toes of unused shoes, in discarded cigarette boxes—even between the pages of books. Sometimes, he moved them twice or three times a day. It became ridiculous. At last, he hid them in the laundry hamper. Minna never did the wash. He did. Dirty shirts and blouses—dirty socks and underwear—but no babies. Safety.

6

Two days after the bones had been found in the tumbled house next door, and two days after the "naked" runner, a party was to be given downtown and neither of them really wanted to go. Kate, however, had insisted.

"You can't let me down," she had said to Minna on the phone. "I'm calling out all the troops. I want every name in the book."

The occasion was the launch of a new novel—written by a neophyte. *But a neophyte of brilliance. Wait until you read it. It will knock your socks off!*

When the book arrived by courier, Bragg regarded it with suspicion. He did not like to read other people's work when he was writing, being afraid he would discover—under someone else's hand—the perfect articulation of the very subject he was struggling with himself.

Minna liked it. *Short, precise and merciless,* she said when she'd finished reading.

"What's it about?" Bragg asked, thinking the plot alone could do no harm.

"It's about an older man who's gay."

Bragg took another sip of wine, saying nothing. Minna was watching him. "Oh," he said.

"Yes. Older, like sixty, Bragg. Not like thirty-five." She was smiling. "And ...?"

"And he wants to have an affair with a younger man." Pause. "Younger, like seventeen." Now, not smiling.

They had been in the living-room—*the drawing-room*—when this conversation took place. Both had been working. Now, they were drinking.

"The story is told from the point of view of the boy. *Death in Venice* in reverse."

"Interesting."

"Yes. And beautifully handled."

"Does one of them walk into the sea at the end?"

"Sort of."

"While the other watches and dies?"

"You could say that."

There was a prolonged and well-thought-out pause, after which Bragg said: "I wouldn't write a gay novel for all the tea in China."

Minna knew this. Bragg had eschewed the subject entirely. He didn't even write gay characters into his stories. None. Minna's novels abounded in them.

"I hate the word *gay*," Bragg said. "It makes it all seem so trite. We didn't end up in Auschwitz because we were *trite,* for God's sake. Somebody took us seriously."

Minna looked at her hands, her fingers extended. She hated the subject—but only for Bragg's sake. She knew she was married to—and in love with—a gay man. But it didn't bother her at all. *Why should it bother me? It would be like saying that* thing between your legs bothers me ... *I'm in love with a man. To hell with the rest.*

"We write what we write," she said that night, when they talked about the Neophyte's novel. "When you want to write about being ...," she hesitated for three seconds, "... homosexual, you will. That's the end of it."

"It's not the end of it. Now there's this new young genius out there waiting to do us all in."

Oh, God—here we go again.

"He's no threat to you, Bragg," Minna said. "No one is a threat to you." She tried to smile. "Not even me."

Bragg himself smiled—at last. "You?" he said. "You couldn't write your way out of a wet paper bag!"

Minna grinned.

"No," she said, "but I bet I could write my way in."

7

Because it was April, it rained. Minna went upstairs to change after supper. They had eaten spaghetti in the kitchen. The book launch was at seven-thirty, which meant they had to drive downtown at seven. "Better get out the umbrellas," she said as she went past Ben on the landing. "Maybe even the rubber boots, from the look of it."

Bragg poured another glass of wine and carried the dishes over to the sink. He was trying to think of some excuse not to go. He hated all events that had to do with writers and writing. *We aren't public figures. We're private*, he said. *Try telling that to Norman Mailer* was Minna's answer.

Up in the twilight, Minna—half undressed—sat on the bed and made a display on the coverlet of what she would carry in her pocketbook. There were certain things—talismans—without which she would not leave the house. The pocketbook itself lay open and waiting; empty. It was made of black velvet and had a gold lining.

Why must you call it a pocketbook? her mother had whined. *Women haven't carried pocketbooks since 1942.*

I will carry one to my death, said Minna.

But why, dear? Why?

Because I like it, Mother. I like the sound of it.

But, Minnie, dear ...

*I LIKE THE SOUND OF IT, MOTHER! AND DON'T CALL
ME MINNIE! I'M NOT A MOUSE!*

Yes, dear.

Minna had to smile. There, amongst the talismans, was a
Mickey Mouse watch. It had been Alma's. It kept perfect time
and when it wasn't in the pocketbook it sat on Minna's bureau
beside a brass-framed photograph of Alma and herself as children. *She was never anything else but a child ...* They wore white
dresses with dreadful puffed sleeves, satin sashes, ribbons in their
hair, and Mary Jane shoes and white socks. They were holding
hands and sitting on a bank of "grass" in a photographer's studio.
A small white "lamb" was also in evidence. Stuffed. Alma was
wearing the watch.

The other talismans were of less sentimental value—but valued,
all the same. A silver lighter from Bragg, inscribed: *To keep our love
alive ...*

Love is a flame, you see.

Yes.

She had been weeping when it was given. Weeping and ill and
wearing a blue flannel bathrobe. That was in the Parkin Institute
of Psychiatric Research during one of Minna's *episodes.* She had
wanted to go home, but the doctor had insisted she stay at the
Parkin for a month. Minna's episodes consisted of panic-driven
outbursts of manic activity which had to be controlled with drugs.

I haven't had one, Bragg, for six years.

You haven't had one since your mother died—that's the truth of it.

Yes.

It had been Minna's mother who first had her committed.

Seventeen years old and totally out of control. *I can't do a thing with her!* Like hair on a bad day. The woman who did not believe in doctors did believe in strait-jackets, so it seemed.

The other talisman was a short string of worry beads—blue stones the size of fingernails, strung on a silver thread. They had been given to Minna by a one-time bag-lady on Queen Street for whom Minna had found a home. *I won't need these, now that I've got a door to close,* the woman had said.

Minna kissed each object as she placed it in the pocketbook. Then she laid a packet of cigarettes beside them and a handkerchief over the lot. Clicking it closed, she kissed the pocketbook itself and held it to her breast. "This is my bag of bones," she said out loud. *All my stillborn children. Alma. Bag-lady. Bragg.*

When Bragg came in a moment later, he found Minna sitting almost in the dark.

"Late," he said. "We'll be late." And turned on the light.

8

"Don't say anything nasty to Marsden, if he's there," Minna said, stepping into the black silk trousers she had bought for the occasion. Marsden was a critic everyone read and detested. Once, when he lavished sudden praise on one of Minna's novels, she had said to Bragg: *something must be terribly wrong. He likes it.*

"He always looks as if he's just had sex at the morgue," Bragg said, tying his tie.

"Yes—but you aren't going to say so, are you."

Bragg persisted. "With someone who's been lying there dead for a week."

"Stop that!" Minna laughed.

"I've heard he keeps one of those life-size rubber dolls in his freezer, so it will be suitably cold when he wants to make use of it."

"Stop!" said Minna. "I can't get my buttons done up."

"That's another thing," said Bragg. "His buttons are always undone. Which is why you know he's just had sex at the morgue."

"*Buttons?*" said Minna. "Whatever happened to zippers?"

"Zippers freeze," said Bragg. "Frozen, they jam—either open or closed. Therefore, he wouldn't be able to get it back in—or out, as the case might be. Ergo: buttons. *The necrophiliac's best friend.*"

"STOP!"

"*Michael Marsden, whom writers dread, screws the living and fucks the dead!*"

Minna, helpless with wine and laughter, sat back down on the bed. "Are you finished?" she said. "How are we ever going to get there? Look at the time! And I'm not even half dressed."

Bragg, who only needed to put on his jacket, got Minna to her feet and helped her into the Chinese silk jacket she kept for special events. It was the one piece of clothing she wore again and again. *Who cares if everyone's seen it before? Red is such a dashing colour. Brave. That's why so many flags have red in them.* Red was certainly the word for it. Scarlet, with blue-thread leaves and lemon-thread birds. Its collar sat up, squared beneath her chin. *It makes me feel as if I'm sober,* she said—because it buttoned her in and she had to stand up straight in order to wear it.

Finally—*there!* She stood beside him, watching them both in the mirror.

"My God, we make a handsome couple."

"True."

She took his arm and pulled him closer, looking up at his profile—his hawk's nose and his tumbled hair.

"Surely you have to be the most beautiful man on earth," she said.

Bragg shook his head. "No," he said. "Thank you—but I'm not."

He did not elaborate.

9

The party was held in a bistro called Le Bistingo on Queen Street. Everyone arrived with a soaked umbrella. One of the waiters took all of these and stood them, folded, in a white enamelled tub in the corner. *Flowers for the dead,* Bragg thought. Minna said to Kate: "I think you've taken the *Death in Venice* motif a little far. Will there be gondolas?"

"Couldn't afford them," Kate said. "You look splendid."

"Thank you. Red becomes me."

"And you, Stuart."

Bragg nodded—distracted. "Kate." *Why had he thought about flowers for the dead?* Maybe it was just in the air. So far, he hadn't seen a single person smiling.

"Our author's not here yet," said Kate. "Typical. Slight case of panic, I suspect. Or perhaps an innate sense of when to make an entrance. Either way, he's half an hour late."

"You certainly have a good turn-out," said Minna, looking for and seeing familiar faces. "If the Neophyte doesn't hurry, he may not find a place to stand."

"Neophyte?"

"Author person."

"Ah, yes. Well—he certainly doesn't write like a neophyte. What did you think?"

"I thought it was splendid. Unpoetic, thank God—and, by some miracle, unpretentious—given its subject matter."

"Stuart?"

"Haven't read it." Seeing Minna's expression, he added, "yet."

Kate gave him one of her dismissive smiles: *you poor pathetic sod.* Bragg looked away as if he hadn't seen.

Michael Marsden was standing about five feet away—pinstriped, bow-tied and balding. He was waving an empty glass in the air, scattering droplets of red wine in all directions while he lectured someone whose back was non-informative to Bragg. She wore a green dress and her hair was the colour of eggplants. Not unattractive. Her earrings looked dangerous—real, not imitation razor blades. Clearly, Marsden was enchanted by this woman. Circe, perhaps, had conquered him at last. He was playing the *doyen-critic* to the hilt, giving her one of his famous obloquies on the subject of why the novel had died.

Having suffered an infusion of gender-driven plots—men gone ape—women gone aper—it might as well be said the novel had been murdered. Now, he said in his high, nasal voice, *we have nigger-books, faggot-books and dyke-books. North-American-Indian-books! Feminist-books and macho-books! Where will it end? and WHEN?*

The last true novelist was Evelyn Waugh and the classic mode went out with him. Out like a light. Amis, père, came close, he would say, *but never quite managed to pull it off ...* Marsden wrote a good deal about *Amis, père et fils,* finding the phrase amusing and clever. Someone, seeking vengeance for yet another negative review, had once sent a letter addressed to *Marsden, Michael—fils of a bitch.*

Watching him, Bragg was wondering why it was that God stood up so often for bastards. They always seemed to win the palm—their voices drowning out the voices of probity and balance.

He smiled. *Probity and balance* had a *Marsdenesque* ring to it. *Honesty and decency* would do just as well, although Bragg was perfectly aware of why he had avoided using such words. They were embarrassments. Anachronisms. Crudities. Signals of naïveté. *The more debased and devious we become,* he thought, *the more we cloud the language with erudition.*

Bragg lifted a glass from a passing tray and looked again at Michael Marsden. His pale, translucent skin was pulled unusually tight across the balloon of his face. Surely, if one more breath of air were to be applied, it would explode. Not only that—Marsden, of all things, appeared to be perspiring.

Can Marsden sweat? Bragg said to Minna in his mind. *Will wonders never cease? And he actually seems to have the hots for one of the living, for a change ...*

The purple-haired woman turned in Bragg's direction, almost as if she had heard what he was thinking. Bragg winced. *Good Lord!* It wasn't a woman at all. It was Alan McKenzie, in drag.

Oh, where is Minna? She was missing the best show in town.

Alan McKenzie wrote light-hearted pieces for various magazines and, from time to time, they were gathered into books which often won awards. They were always trashed by Marsden. Alan, it so happened, was not a homosexual. He was merely a man in drag. An angry man—and dangerous. His razor blades flashed in the light as he made his way to Bragg's side.

"Don't say anything, for God's sake," he said. "I think I've got him hooked."

Bragg said nothing—but nodded. Then he said: "what do I call you?"

"Sylvia."

"Who is Sylvia—what is she?"

"You've got it, Pontiac." Sylvia-Alan raised her glass and drank.

Bragg said: "are you actually going to bed him?"

"Are you kidding? *Please.* If I ever do get to lose my virginity, I want to lose it to a human being. *But*—I do intend to give Mister Marsden the shock of his fucking life."

"How?"

"You'll see. At least, you'll hear."

"You're going to do it offstage?"

"Sort of. In the men's room. You can come and watch, if you want to. I think the moment will deserve an audience."

"As long as you aren't going to ..."

"What? Go down on him? I'd rather go down on the *Titanic.*"

Bragg laughed.

Minna arrived. She was carrying, besides her glass and an unlit cigarette, a bottle of Côtes du Rhone.

"You were laughing. I thought I'd better find out why ..." She stopped and stared. "Alan ..?"

"Sylvia," said Bragg.

"But it's ..."

"Sylvia Alan," said Alan.

"Why?"

"You'll see."

"No she won't," said Bragg.

"True." Then, to Minna: "Stuart will tell you later."

Minna said: "I can't wait. Meanwhile, could one of you light this cigarette? I've lost my pocketbook."

"I hope to God your wallet wasn't in it."

"Not my wallet, no. But Alma's watch and my lovely silver lighter, Bag-lady beads and a handkerchief I rather liked. Oh, dear ..."

"Never mind. We'll find it."

Suddenly, Sylvia Alan started to move away. "Now," she said.

Bragg lighted Minna's cigarette and followed.

10

In the washroom, Marsden already stood at the urinals with his back to the sinks. Sylvia Alan cautioned Bragg to be silent and preceded him. Hanging back in the shadows, Bragg saw Marsden turn his head and nod at the person beside him. Then:

"Sylvia! Dear one—you can't come in here!"

"I had to follow you," Sylvia said, using Alan's voice. "I love you—and I want you, here and now."

"Your voice ..." said Marsden.

"What about my voice?"

"It's so ... so ..."

"All voices deepen when people want sex."

"Yes, but ..."

"Don't you understand? I want you to make love to me."

"But ..."

"First I have to take a leak." Saying this, Alan lifted Sylvia's emerald skirts chest high, revealing his naked backside to Bragg—and a good deal more to Marsden.

Marsden stared, his hands flying up from his crotch to cover his face. "Oh!" he said. "OH! OH! OH!"

And then he screamed.

Everyone heard him. The entire, crowded restaurant. And everyone saw him emerge from the men's room pursued by a woman fuming at his back. "This is an outrage!" the woman cried. "An absolute fucking outrage! You never told me you wanted me to do it like that!"

Do what like what?

It was never said.

What did get said was: "you had me put on this dress! *You* chose these earrings! And you gave me *this*!"

To everyone's astonishment but Bragg's and Minna's, Alan McKenzie took the purple wig from his head and threw it at Michael Marsden.

Marsden, of course, would have preferred to escape the building altogether, but he was stopped in his tracks—still carrying the wig—halfway across the room.

"Michael!" It was Kate. She might have been calling a dog to heel. "Stop right there."

He did.

11

"I have something I want to read to you," Kate said.

An arena had been framed, with Marsden at the centre and everyone else around the sides. Even the umbrellas, leaning forward in their enamelled tub, seemed prepared to listen. It was suddenly so quiet the traffic could be heard on Queen Street.

Kate stepped into the circle, shaking out some printed pages and putting on her glasses.

"This has just arrived by courier," she said. "It will explain to all of you why our author is not here tonight—and why he will not be ..."

Oh, dear, Minna thought. *Another casualty.* She looked at Bragg and thought: *don't let this hurt him, whatever it is.* He was so edgy these days—nervy—ready for a fall.

Kate explained that what she was about to read had been sent—*by some well-meaning idiot*—to the Neophyte, saying: *it might be best if you see this before it appears in print ...*

Well, no—as Kate said: *it had not been best.* It was, in fact, devastating. Well-Intentioned had got hold of the piece because he worked at the magazine where it was to be published. Sending it, he had no real knowledge of the man who would be reading it—only of the man who wrote it: Marsden. A neophyte is, after all, just that—someone whose talents, however fine, are fragile. Having just broken free of the chrysalis, the wings are not yet strong—there is moisture on them still. Flight is impossible.

"*The world,*" Kate read, "*little needs and little wants yet one more version of* Death in Venice ..."

How's that for openers?

It was Marsden at his best—and worst. The killer with his set of brilliant knives, honed to within a fare-thee-well. A surgeon might have used them to save a life. Not Marsden. *Any death will do,* someone had once said of him, *so long as the kill is his.*

Now, that evening at Le Bistingo, there was a difference. Not that a death did not take place. A book, its author and its subject were butchered by an expert—but the effect was curious. In Marsden's presence, the words he had written took on colours they would not have had in print. They revealed him as he was—not as he was imagined. Petty—not monstrous. Mean—not clever. Minna, still in mourning for her bag of bones, stood with her finger stuck in the bottle of Côtes du Rhone, letting it hang against her thigh while she smoked a pensive cigarette. *The cigarette is not pensive, my dear—the listener is ...*

It went on and on. And on. Marsden had used the publication of the Neophyte's novel as the springboard for an extended attack on homosexuals, homosexuality, publishing, publishers and novels by *freaks* (his word). He decried *the current emphasis on homosexual themes and variations* and also publishers for having *surrendered to queer culture* and *the gay lobby.* He took a swipe at Gide and another swipe at Genet—and a swipe at France for having harboured them. (He hated everything French.) He then went on to describe *the pathetic state of public taste* in sexual matters and *the decline of cultural values that had left the door ajar for anyone to enter ...*

Minna turned away. Where was Bragg?

He had disappeared.

12

Earlier, while he was doing the dishes by twilight, Bragg had known he had no desire to come to this affair. Still, he had also known he must—for Minna's sake, because of Kate Dance. *I will pretend,* he thought then, *not to be there. I will pretend I am sitting on the hill ...*

This way, he avoided most of what Marsden was postulating in Kate's voice. That it offended him went without saying. That it frightened him was equally certain. What he had not expected was that it would anger him. Deeply. Marsden always made a person testy. You never came away from one of his pieces without at least thinking: *someone should kill the son of a bitch.* But over time you learned not to let him anger you profoundly. Otherwise, whole days could be lost in composing diatribes against him. This, however, was different. Hearing it, while watching Marsden's moonlike face, made it personal to a degree Bragg could not have imagined. *He's attacking me,* he thought. *He's attacking who and what I am. It's Auschwitz time again. He's saying we should go away and be gone entirely.*

Then he thought: *how can someone be saying this, expounding it in print?*

Be careful, Bragg, Minna warned in his mind. *Remember freedom of speech ...*

Bragg moved back towards the bar—the bar at its farthest end, near the windows where Queen Street gleamed beyond the glass, washed and redolent with spring, rain-wet and free of confinement.

Across the road, beyond the cars, the streetcars and the passing parade of umbrellas, he could see a dress shop where something red was on display. Minna-red. Scarlet. Hopelessly alive and yearning to be seen.

Bragg turned away.

Why was he so afraid of being seen? Identified. Known. Of wearing red.

From *the hilltop*, he looked out over the room.

Kate was reading now from the final page. It was excruciating. Marsden had outdone himself in his bid to put an end to *the triumph of queer culture*. Not only had he made a fool of himself, he had upped the ante in behalf of the gay lobby. And ...

What?

He had shown himself to be pathetic.

There he stood, baited by his own words, melting under their heat. *Marsden, yes, can sweat.* It was sad. He was human—and even he had not known it. For one entirely crazy moment, Bragg was tempted to cross the room and put his arm around him. His pinstripe suit no longer fitted him. It sagged and drooped and hung like a piece of mismanaged tailoring. All the buoyant air had left his face, and its shape had been reduced to a pencilled outline—an unfilled circle waiting for a child with crayons to give it life. Sylvia's wig hung down from his hands like something won on the midway—garish and overstuffed.

Well. He would have to begin again. *Like all the rest of us.*

Bragg turned sideways. Thirsty.

He approached the bar. And stopped.

There stood his runner. Fully clothed.

"Can I help you?"

Yes.

No.

"Yes."

"What would you like? It's on the house, as you know."

Bragg ordered a double Scotch—a drink he hadn't had for over a year. His heart hurt. His diaphragm had a lump in it. Something—what?—was going to happen.

When the young man returned—white-coated, long-fingered, smelling of lemons—he set Bragg's drink on the bar and placed a small glass pitcher filled with water beside it. "I think I know who you are," he said. "And I think I may have something you want."

No. Don't do this, Bragg almost said aloud. "Oh?"

"Yes. You're Stuart Bragg, aren't you."

Bragg nodded and drank—without adding water. "That's right," he said.

Had the boy—*he was a boy*—looked up from the bottom of the hill and seen him after all?

"I found this," the runner said. "It had fallen over the edge, into the sink. I looked inside—I'm sorry. But I wanted to know whose it was. And I saw the inscription on the lighter. I think it belongs to your wife."

Bragg sat down on a stool.

"Yes," he said. "Thank you."

It was Minna's pocketbook. Her bag of bones.

Bragg made a play for a successful gesture—and failed. He had wanted to light a cigarette as if nothing had happened—just as if he hadn't thought he was going to die. But he dropped his lighter onto the floor and couldn't bear to lean so far down to retrieve it. If he had, he knew he would have fallen.

"Never mind," said the boy. "Use this."

For Minna—To keep our love alive—Love, B.

The flame wavered.

Bragg inhaled.

"My name," the boy said, "is Colin Marsh. I hope we meet again."

13

That night, Bragg slept in the sunroom with Ben. *I'll be working,* he said to Minna, *and don't want to disturb you.*

Fine.

And it was. Minna didn't need him. Not then. She would—but later.

When Bragg had handed her the pocketbook as they left Le Bistingo, she had burst into tears and all the way home she wept.

We almost lost each other, she had thought in the car. *We almost lost each other to the old despair.*

Now, in the great double bed they most often shared, Minna crouched in the dark with her knees drawn up to her chin and a wine glass in her hand. Beside her, on the pillow—dear as a sleeping lover—the pocketbook sat open, its contents removed and displayed beside it.

The street lamps provided all the light she could bear. They spread a kind of theatrical moonlight over everything around her.

Marsden had been strung up by the heels. *He will never trouble us again.* Something had been killed by what he'd written—but something else had survived. The Neophyte, in his despair, might have felt he was destroyed, but he hadn't been. Others knew that, and he would come to know it in time. *If he could just get through this moment ...*

Minna looked down at the objects spread on the pillow. *Alma. Bag-lady. Bragg.* All her stillborn children.

Gone. And not gone.

She picked up the silver lighter and lighted a cigarette.

It still works.

Hah!

She smiled.

That boy ... the bartender ... Bragg had liked him.

Good.

She had liked him, too.

Colin Marsh. *Sounds like a place in the wilderness.*

He was coming to dinner next week—though Bragg didn't know it yet. *A person has to do something for someone who finds her bag of bones!*

Babies.

One day.

People kill them so easily. Wrap them in towels. Put them in garbage bags. Leave them in dumpsters. Plaster them over inside the walls. Kill them with reviews. The slaughter of the innocents.

But other babies, still unborn, survive.

Don't they.

Don't they.

Yes.

I'm going to have a baby, Bragg. I'm going to have a dozen babies—and they'll all be yours.

One day.

Come as You Are

1

AND NOW, the dreaded Hallowe'en.

Bragg, who hated children, and Minna, who adored them, were a house divided. On Hallowe'ens past, Minna had tried to persuade Bragg to answer the door at least once. *You're missing the most divine entertainment, my dear. Angels disguised as monsters.*

Bragg had said: *what you mean is monsters showing their true colours.*

This year, things were different. Colin Marsh had come to live at number 141 Collier Street and the house divided had three, not two, divisions. Col was Bragg's lover—a runner who no longer ran, a bartender who no longer tended bar. He was *studying*—a euphemism for floundering—wondering who he was.

Despite the tension of the moment, it was basically a happy household. Minna thrived on intrigue, argument and interfering in other people's lives. Bragg thrived on privacy. His favourite fellow resident was Ben, his dog. Like Bragg, Ben divided his night-time loyalties between Col's bed and Minna's. His presence on either, however, did not necessarily coincide with Bragg's. Ben could not abide a nightmare. Whenever the sleep-talk started to escalate to shouts and murmurs, he was down and gone—which usually meant leaving Bragg. Bragg dreamt most. Col, least. Minna's dreams and nightmares occurred by daylight.

And now, the dreaded Hallowe'en.

Col had suggested he and Bragg should attend a friend's costume party. Bragg said: *no.* Minna said: *if you go to the party, Bragg, you won't have to answer the door. There won't be a child in sight.*

"I can't stand faggots," Bragg said. "Worst of all are drag queens. The whole damn place will be crawling with them. *Slithering!* Batting their silly eyes and wiggling their stupid bums. Not a chance. I wouldn't dream of it."

Minna winked at Col.

"Okay," she said. "Col and I will go. I'll play the man."

"Like hell you will."

"So. Col goes alone. He meets a handsome stranger and doesn't come home. You want that?"

"Of course not."

"Without you there to stop him, he'll drink too much—meet the handsome stranger—get laid and end up with gay cancer."

Bragg looked at Col. Col, who was learning how to take part in Minna's games, gave a shrug and sipped his wine.

"AIDS," Bragg said. "It's called AIDS, now."

"So what," Minna said. "Stupid name. Meaningless."

"It stands for Acquired Immune Deficiency Syndrome."

"I know what what it stands for. But it's still gay cancer. And it can kill you. You want that?"

Bragg stubbed a cigarette.

Dinner over, they were still seated at table—the table in the tiny den where they ate together. Minna had long ago commandeered the dining-room as her office. She wrote in there, beyond the closed French doors, her back hunched above her papers, while General Booth of the Salvation Army glared at her from the opposite wall. General Booth, bearded and uniformed, severe, austere, eternally angry—had been one of Minna's finds in a secondhand store on Queen Street. *I like his eyes,* she had told Bragg. *They tell me not to give up.*

"Gay cancer scares the shit out of me," Minna said. "Jesus, Bragg, don't fuck around."

"You know I don't."

"You, too, Col. Stay away from strange men."

"I can hardly do that. I'm living with Bragg."

Minna laughed. Bragg did not.

Beneath the table, Ben rolled over on his back and let Bragg rub his stomach with his toes.

"If we went," Bragg said, "what costume would you wear?"

"You mean we'll go?"

"*If,* I said. Only if."

Minna waited.

Col said: "a drag queen dressed as a college boy."

Minna roared.

"You can wear my false eyelashes and lipstick. A perfect

scream—with a crew cut! And a southern drawl! I'll lend you my highest heels. A divine idea."

Col turned to Bragg. "Stuart?"

"What?"

"You. What would you wear?"

"Me?" Bragg said. "I'd wear what I always wear to parties. Shirt. Tie. Grey flannels. Blazer."

"But that's not a costume," said Minna. "That's no *disguise.*"

"You think not? I think it's perfect. *THE STRAIGHT MAN WHO SLEEPS WITH BOYS!* What else would he wear?"

Minna said nothing.

Col said: "I'm not a boy."

Bragg poured more wine.

"We'll go on one condition," he said. "When I say it's time to leave—we leave. Pronto."

Minna sighed. "Does this mean you'll be home before dark?"

"No," said Bragg. "But home before the witching hour."

2

Mercy McIsaac had entered Minna's life through what Minna called the *side door.* The *front door* was street people. The *back door* was family. *Keep them out of sight,* she said. All, except Alma—her sister who had died. Alma needed no doors or windows. She came in down the chimney—not unlike Santa Claus. Not unlike soot. *The soot of memory. Grime of the past,* Minna called it. The horror, the sadness, the madness a person could not wash away.

Mercy McIsaac had come through the side door of commerce. So to speak. She had been hired five years ago to spread the good word about Minna's novels. *I have no family,* Mercy had said. *My only relations are public.* Minna adored her. When they first met, Mercy was thirty-something years old, and had just survived a bout with cancer. At that time she was a skinny redhead whose hair style was *shaggy dog* short and banged to the eyes. *I wear my hair as a parasol, Min.* Her body was the handle—*the stick by which I prop the best part of me—my head—above the crowd.*

Not having family—not having cultivated many friends with whom she was comfortable—Mercy had fallen under Minna's spell the first day they worked together. She was good at her job—extremely good. Before Minna knew it, her name and the titles of her books were everywhere. Prior to Mercy, Minna Joyce had been *well known.* Now, she was famous. Mercy had given her commercial edge. *The reading public has to want* you—*not just your books.*

"I could do wonders for Bragg," she once said to Minna.

"Bragg doesn't want to be liked" was Minna's reply. "He thrives on his own obscurity."

"He shouldn't be obscure. His work is beautiful."

"Don't tell him that," Minna said. "He'd wonder what was wrong with it."

"But it *is.* Beautiful."

"I know that. But accolades distress him. *Not why I write,* he says."

"What about your success. Does it distress him?"

"Not in the least. He knows I'm good. He knows who I am. He loves me. Trouble is, he won't acknowledge how good he is himself—or who he is—and especially that *I* love *him.* The poor man lives in terror of success. It might mean he'd have to admit he'd done something right"

"What a dreadful way to live."

"He survives."

3

Hallowe'en that year—it was 1984—fell on a Wednesday.

Bragg and Col left for their party at seven, having eaten a meal consisting of rye bread sandwiches containing bacon and tomato—*no lettuce.*

"Lettuce is nothing but green water," Bragg said. "I'm not about to go to a fag party where I have to pee ten times."

Using the toilet in other people's houses or in public places was anathema to Bragg. *Everyone will think I'm trying to pick them up.* Standing at a urinal was agony. He always used a cubicle. *If you shake it more than twice, everyone thinks you're jerking off.*

"If you shake it more than twice, you *are* jerking off," said Col.

"Not in my books," said Bragg.

"In your books," Minna said, "no one jerks off—including the reader. That's what people want, Bragg—a good excuse to amuse themselves."

"Oh? You think so?"

"No. I know so."

"Really. Fascinating. You mean if I see you carrying *Watership Down* into the john, I'll know there's something going on?"

"Very funny. On the other hand—there are all those naked rabbits."

Bragg, as promised, wore a shirt and tie, grey flannels and a blue blazer. Col wore chinos, lipstick, a button-down shirt, stiletto heels, a cotton jacket and Minna's false eyelashes. He also wore a pearl-drop earring. *Simply sensational,* said Minna. *Absolutely gorgeous.* And then: *you, too, Col. I love the hair.*

Col had sprayed his crew cut till it stood straight up. This gave him the look of cartoon amazement—making it seem that someone had just said *boo!*

"Give anyone I know my love," Minna said as they left the living-room, making for the hall. "And just remember—no strange men."

"Goodbye."

"Goodbye."

Poor baby, Minna thought as she watched Bragg close the door. *You'd think he was going to be guillotined.*

Ten minutes later, Mercy McIsaac arrived and Bragg and Col were forgotten.

4

Minna set out a twin-set of Côtes du Rhone.

"Bragg and I always drink from separate bottles," she said. She had pondered setting out one Côtes du Rhone and one Beaujolais, but had thought: *I mustn't. After all, a man's wine is a man's wine. And mine is mine.* She also set out two of the Waterford goblets that had been among Grandmother Joyce's prized possessions.

Mercy arrived with a velvet toque pulled over her ears. "Cold," she said. "It's cold out there. The kiddies will freeze." The hat was well known to Minna. Mercy had no other. It was her trademark.

"You look like death," Minna said. And smiled.

Mercy said nothing and handed Minna her overcoat—a ratty old raccoon. The toque, she retained. Purple, with a silver-threaded arabesque motif that gave it a Persian look. "I couldn't find a mask I liked," she said, "so this is all the costume you get."

"No kiddies yet," said Minna, "but help yourself if you're inclined." She gestured to the bowls of miniature candy bars, jelly beans and bags of Planter's peanuts—Mister Peanut staring up from every one.

"No thanks," said Mercy. "I always drink on an empty stomach."

In the living-room, Minna started the fire she had already laid.

"I long for the days of coal," she said. "You remember them? Big huge chunks of cannel coal, vast—like *Titanic* icebergs—shedding their slabs into the fire, burning blue and green and yellow. And the smell! It was heaven."

"We always burned wood. Birch was my favourite."

"Where'd you grow up? Montreal, right?"

"Westmount."

"Oooh! Get you! I had the Toronto equivalent. Rosedale. I hated it."

"Not me," said Mercy. "I loved every minute of it. Not that we were greatly rich. Just that we were Anglos."

"*Les maudits anglais ...*"

"*Oui.* We lived on Thornhill Avenue. There were trees."

"Yes. And burning leaves for Hallowe'en. The whole street smelled of maple and apple smoke." She smiled. "And birch ..."

"Not any more."

"Yeah," said Minna. "Leaf burning ain't allowed no more. Good ol' Toronto—where *nothing* is allowed."

Mercy laughed. "Montreal's the same."

The doorbell rang.

"Customer number one," said Minna, and went out into the hall. "Drink up, slowpoke. I'm nearly halfway through my first bottle. You've barely started."

5

"Whose party is this?" Bragg asked. He was driving.

"Man called Nellie Nelson," said Col. He adjusted his earring. Tighter.

"Never heard of him."

"Well, no wonder. Not your purview. I've known him for years. Does make-up at the CBC. Television."

"Not radio?"

"Pooh on you. Of course not radio."

"Well, you never know. That sportscaster—Gordon Anderson? He sounds pretty fey to me."

Col laughed. "Gordon Anderson has three kids, a ravishing wife and a stint with the Junior A. Saint Mike's. Almost made it to the NHL—but had a bum knee."

"*Bum-knee* so called. More likely got the boot for staring in the locker-room."

"God, you're cynical. Even worse, in spite of who you are and who I am and what we do—you don't like gays."

"That's right."

Col gave him a look. Bragg wasn't smiling. Col looked away.

"Who's apt to be there?" Bragg asked. "Any predictions?"

"Can't really tell. Not in terms of people you'd know."

"But lots of people you'd know."

"Probably. Don't forget, bartending introduces you to everyone."

Bragg made a corner just before the light turned and muttered:
right—right again—then left.

"When I saw you running," he said, "you know—the first time
I saw you before we met—I wanted you to be queer—but I didn't
think you were. Too many macho symbols. Too much macho
behaviour. Then I find you tending bar at a book launch and I still
can't believe you're queer. Now, we're going to a party with you
in mascara, wearing an earring. It's not that I was fooled. That
couldn't matter less—and, by the way, thank God I was. But ...
Have you been living this life full-time or part-time? Half in—half
out—or what?"

"Full-time," said Col. "Just like you—but more committed."

"You bloody bitch!" Bragg said—but he was laughing.

"It's true. You're the queerest queer I've ever met. In bed, you
prove that. There isn't a square inch of me you haven't ravished,
and yet ...," he shrugged, "... there you sit in that damned blue
blazer. Minna is still the centre of your life. You still talk *straight.*
You never tell gay jokes. You never rejoice in male beauty—not
out loud, you don't, and certainly never in your writing. But,
Jesus, Stuart—I've never had my nipples twisted or my ass
fingered the way you do. Never. I mean—the other night, I
thought: now I know what they mean by *ass-ault.*"

Bragg was silent. Then he said: "you and Minna are all I have that's alive."

"You left out Ben," said Col.

Bragg laughed.

Col said: "you also left out you."

"Me?" said Bragg. "I'm not alive. Revived, from time to time—maybe. But not alive."

"Liar."

"Try me."

"You forget, Mister Bragg—Stu honey—Stuart darling—Bragg baby. I already have."

They had almost reached their destination.

Col said: "I don't have burn marks for nothing, my dear. I don't have these scars by chance. I'm covered with your fingerprints. Covered from head to toe and back again on the other side."

"You sound just like Minna," said Bragg.

"I know," Col said. "I know I do. I've been practising."

6

Twelve children, so far. All of them known—none of them recognized.

Bragg could be right. *You are what you choose.* His blue blazer—Annie Nugent's skeleton.

"Who's Annie Nugent?" Mercy asked. They were still on their second bottle of Côtes du Rhone, though Minna—*of course, my dear*—was deeper into hers than Mercy.

"Kid down the block," she said. "Thirteen, maybe. Twelve.

Forty pounds overweight, because she looks at a chocolate bar. I almost wept for her, standing there in her skeleton costume—five-foot-two—a hundred and seventy pounds."

Mercy stared at the fire.

"Can I offer it another log?" she said.

"Of course you can. You can offer it anything you like."

For a moment, they were silent. Mercy laid a piece of birch-wood—bark unravelling, loosened, peeling down—on the glowing remains of the applewood that had preceded it.

"We burn so fast," she said. "We burn so fast."

Minna did not reply. She was thinking: *the whole street smelled of maple and apple smoke. And birch. Leaf smoke.* Verboten. *Childhood. Children. Child.*

Mercy was staring at the fire.

"That boyfriend of yours," Minna said. "Fred? Is it serious?"

"Yes."

"And will you ..."

"We live together—yes. We won't get married."

"What about kids?"

"Nope." Mercy shook her head and reached for her glass. "No," she said. And drank. Then she said: "I've had one pass at death. All that chemo shit. Lost one breast—and all my hair to boot. Thank you—no. I'll pass."

Minna crossed her legs and waited.

Mercy smiled. "Who needs another orphan?" she said.

Minna shrugged. *Me,* she almost said. And then: *shut up.*

Mercy said: "what about you and kids?"

"Don't I wish," said Minna. "Don't I wish. But—Bragg don't wish."

"*Does not.*"

"Do not. *Don't.* We speak dialect here. Just in case people think we're civilized. Know what I mean? Just in case it looks and sounds like a civilized household: *man, woman, dog.*"

"And friend."

"Friend?"

"Col."

"Colin? That ain't no friend. That's my knife."

"You don't like him?"

"Sure I like him. Love him, in fact. Very nice chap. Clean—quiet—helps with the dishes. I just don't want to lose my husband. Get *cut off* at the pass."

"Bragg will never leave you."

"No. But I may leave him. *Have* to leave him."

"I don't believe that for a minute."

"Well—you'd better."

"Why? Because of Col?"

"No. Because I want a baby."

"Go out and buy one."

Minna made a face. "Don't think I haven't considered it," she said. "Though not the way you think. Not one adopted. Has to be mine—and so ... I've talked to Doctor Reese about artificial insemination."

"Jesus."

"Well—no. Jesus is not available." Minna drank. "I want Bragg's babies," she said. "Bragg's. Only Bragg's. But the way I'm beginning to feel, I'd settle for Charlie Manson's babes."

The doorbell rang.

"There he is," said Mercy.

"You think you could bear to go?" Minna said. "I have to pee like you wouldn't believe." She stood up.

Mercy said: "you're asking me to let in Charlie Manson?"

"That's right."

Minna went through the dining-room all the way to the kitchen, down the back stair and into the frigid loo. Its light was harsh and lonely, Minna always thought, as though somehow they had consigned the room to limbo. *One toilet—one sink—one bulb*—a perfect description of hell.

Beyond the door, Mercy could see a child who appeared to be wearing adult clothes. A small green hat and a tailored coat. Tweed—blue-green and very smart.

Smart was a word that Mercy's mother had used. *That's a smart dress. That's a smart suit. That's a smart boy ...*

How did this constitute a costume?

I just asked someone to run it up—you know—it only cost nine hundred dollars and I thought: why not? Hallowe'en comes but once a year.

Rich kids.

Mercy pulled at the door. It was locked. Once opened, it revealed a child whose appearance, for all its couturier elegance, was more than somehow alarming. The mask was surreal—a perfect replica of some-one nearing seventy—not exaggerated—not grotesque—just aged.

"Hello."

"Hello."

"I'm just a visitor," Mercy said. "Mrs Bragg is ... in the kitchen."

The incarnation of age was carrying a plastic shopping bag. *Loblaws.*

Mercy turned to reach for the candy bars and peanuts.

Next thing she knew, the child was standing beyond her in the vestibule.

"All I'm doin' is deliverin'," she said.

Irish.

Mercy let the candy fall back into its bowl. She did not know how to deal with her expression. The voice that spoke with such a brogue was not the voice of a child at all. It was the voice of a woman well along in years.

Some kids may be terrific actors, Mercy thought, *but this is phenomenal.*

"Yes?" she said—and turned. "Delivering what?"

"I'm Ida Murphy," the *child* said. "I'm bringin' Minna's new dress."

"Oh, I see," said Mercy.

Ida Murphy was four-foot-eight—sixty-nine years old—and had made the dress Minna had worn at her christening.

Minna called her Spud.

7

Nellie Nelson wore a red dress in which, if the truth be told, he looked remarkably at home. Not like a man in drag at all.

"I stole it from Wardrobe," he said. "Two years ago, it was worn by Anne Murray. Suddenly I've discovered I can sing ..." He demonstrated. *Snowbird.*

"Heavens," said Col. "That's very good."

"Thank you," said Nellie. "The problem is ... I'm left with one big question."

"Yes?"

"I suspect the voice may come with the dress. There are all these *thingies* sewn up the sides. Do you see? And I think—I mean, I *know*—there's a *very* strange sensation—kind of a tingling—when I sing. Makes me wonder ... has anyone *seen* Anne Murray lately? Or—am I wearing her?"

Bragg—for Bragg—was not so lucky. He got trapped in a corner with an older man who delivered what amounted to a treatise on the subject of the penis and its size. He was so erudite, he might have been an academic.

In ancient times ... one paragraph began. *In various Amazonian tribes* ... began another. Also: *the phallus is all we have left of certain statues* ... And: *it cannot go without comment that Picasso was the only twentieth-century artist to portray the penis as it is, in its true dimensions....*

Bragg, whose mind had wandered, paused when he heard this pronouncement. Unavoidably, he conjured an image of his own penis. *Does he mean* small *as it is—or* large *as it is?*

There was no one there he knew—barring Col. And the atmosphere of parties—any party, anywhere, given for whatever reason—left him feeling like a stranger to the human race. *Baffled by the blatting,* he once wrote in his journal, following a particularly galling event from which he had come home voiceless. Not that he had said much, but everything he had said had to be shouted.

It wasn't that Bragg took no interest in other people—or in how the world around them fared at their hands. Or in how they touched one another with their lives—touched or remained untouching because they refused to reach across the space between themselves and others. He saw all that and he knew all that—saw it and knew it, but turned away for fear that he himself would be seen. Seen and known.

He looked around the room. The decor was acceptable—one or two rather good paintings hung on Hunter green walls and a mass of drawings, vaguely erotic. The furniture might have been chosen by a set designer and more than likely had been. If you work *in the business*, you take advantage of everyone else's superior talents. But the people ...

All they live for is their queerdom. Nothing else defines them. Nothing else, apparently, *tells them who they are.*

Col came out of the throng with a man in tow who wore nothing but a sequined jock strap.

You like jock straps, Bragg—don't complain.

"This is Henry Albanese," Col said. "He wants to meet you."

"How do you do?"

"Not well, since I read your last book."

"Oh? Why is that?"

"I saw myself," said the man in the jock strap. "You write too well."

Bragg was at a loss. He had never written—not once—about his passion for jock straps, hard bodies and short hair—all of which Henry Albanese possessed and all of which he brandished. Brandished, along with his dreadful sibilance, floating hands and bottleful of cologne.

"I just sat there and wept," Henry said. "It was just so revealing.

That bit about the woman—I forget her name—but the woman who wanted the baby ..."

"Jennifer."

"Yes. That bit about the man she loved who was impotent and couldn't give her one ... That was me, Mister Bragg. That was me."

Bragg looked around for escape. Col was standing there unavailable. Halfway through what Henry Albanese had to say, he had begun to eavesdrop on another conversation—leaving Bragg stranded.

Henry Albanese said: "I was married, you see. Very much in love—but quite incapable of love-making. Just like your person ..."

"Jason."

"Jason, yes. Jennifer and Jason." Henry's eyes wandered to one side. He fought back tears—too much to drink, perhaps—and when he looked at Bragg again, Bragg was devastated. All the self-pity and self-importance had faded from Henry's expression. The tears that had started were stemmed and had retreated to their reservoir. "I told my wife I hated her," he said. "*Something* had to be said. I was so ashamed of my failure—my impotence—that I had to make her think it was her fault—not mine. And, of course, disaster followed. I had never done anything in all my life as cruel as that—or as selfish. And she ran away and I knew I would never see her again. Which I didn't."

And?

Henry Albanese scratched himself just below his left nipple. Bragg then noted for the first time the nails painted scarlet and a multiplicity of silver rings.

"I trust that somehow you were reconciled," Bragg said. "A letter, at least." This is what happened in his story, "The Last Straw," to which Henry Albanese had referred.

"No," Henry told him. "No reconciliation. Nothing. She went out west to Vancouver—met a man and was pregnant. Next thing I heard, she was dead. And the man. And the unborn child. Accident victims. Killed by a truck."

"I'm sorry."

"Thank you, but it's okay. I mean, it's okay because at least she knew she was going to have a child. But—your story—that man—the man—Jason whoever—the one in love with Jennifer—that man reminded me so painfully of me that I had to ask you: is it true, or did I simply make it up between the lines? Was he queer? The book doesn't say so, but I wondered."

Bragg thought about it. Jason had not been *queer*, but merely impotent. It had been impotence he had been writing about and its power to destroy relationships because people have to make up reasons for impotence—personal—personality reasons. Love-hate relations. *My fault—your fault.* That had been the subject under Bragg's hand when he wrote "The Last Straw." But now, he did not know what to say.

Bragg glanced at Col, who had now entirely departed his company even though he stood not three feet away. No help there. No help—and no answers. At last, Bragg said: "I think you may have told me something that perhaps I didn't know about my story."

Henry's expression brightened.

Bragg said: "I thought I knew all there was to know about Jason. Jennifer, too. But now, I can see I was wrong."

"He was queer. *Is.*"

"No. I didn't say that. Only that I didn't recognize all the possibilities."

That was the end of it. Someone came and clapped a hand on Henry's naked shoulder. "YOU!" an explosive voice declared. "YOU SEQUINED BITCH!" And Henry was led away.

Bragg was sweating. It was time to leave. He turned to Col and said: *now.*

As they went to the door, Bragg got out his handkerchief and dabbed his forehead and neck.

Close call, he thought. *Too close.*

He was thinking of Henry Albanese. And he was thinking: *Jesus. I almost liked him.*

8

"After nine o'clock," Minna said, "business starts dropping off."

The doorbell rang.

"Wrong," said Minna. "It starts pulling up." She moved towards the door. "Maybe you could heave another faggot on the fire."

Mercy laughed. "I guess you don't say that to Bragg."

"I guess I do. He loves it. Roars. Loves it even more when I ask him to bring another faggot in from the cold—meaning from the wood pile in the backyard." She headed for the vestibule.

By now, there had been almost thirty children—maybe more. Minna had lost count. The bowls of candy bars and jelly beans were nearly empty. All the little bags of Planter's Peanuts were gone. No more *Mister Peanut.*

On her way, she paused to look at the new dress in the hall mirror. *Green, for Miss Murphy,* she thought. *Spud's dress. Very becoming.* She pulled a little at the collar, plunging her fingers into her cleavage. *Feels good, too. Looks good—feels good—is good.*

Satisfied, she went to the door.

There was a figure there on the porch. Somewhat unnerving under the light. A trifle large for a child.

A whole lot too large.

She could hear Mercy poking at the fire and the sound of a weighty log being placed. Then she heard the sound of wine being poured.

Suddenly, Minna realized how tired she was—how long the day had been and how many trips for tricksters she had made through the evening. Plus the afternoon's writing and the morning's *pensées*—ruminations—decisions: *this in and that out* of yesterday's work. It was time to stop and bring an end to Hallowe'en.

If the person on the porch had been a child, he would have been a giant. Dressed in what appeared to be rather expensive leather, he was five-foot-ten—Bragg's height—if he wasn't taller.

Boots. Trousers. Zippered jacket. Gauntlets—not gloves—all black and shiny. Plus a biker's hat. And a red bandanna, serving as a mask, pulled across the lower half of the face.

Minna studied him and paused.

Could be someone I know.

Could be someone's parent. After all, Hallowe'en isn't always just for kids ...

And yet ...

Mister Hell's Angel doesn't have a bag for goodies.

She watched his eyes.

He watched back, unblinking.

Minna reached for the lock. She always kept the door locked until she knew who was there. The bevelled glass, full length, was inches thick, revealing every corner of the porch, the steps and the walk beyond.

Once the door was opened, it let in a draught of frigid air, tinged with Mercy's wood smoke—plus the exhaust fumes from the Mays' Volvo, just departing from the driveway opposite.

"Yes?" said Minna.

The figure did not move.

"Trick," Minna said, "or treat?"

The figure did not move

"Maybe you don't know how to play Hallowe'en," said Minna, smiling. "The way I play it, people talk to each other."

The figure still did not move.

Minna shivered, alarmed. This was not *Hallowe'en*—this was downright sinister. The person, not having moved a muscle, was simply staring at her. *Eyes like something dead,* she thought. *Something found in the woods or washed up on the shore. A corpse stare.* The lack of a mouth was also disconcerting. He looked, Minna thought, like one of those nightmare figures she had dreamt whose lips were sewn together and whose eyes were sewn open.

"Speak," she said, "or I'm going back inside."

There was no reply.

Minna turned and started through the door.

She had made it almost all the way when she felt the back of her dress being dragged and torn.

Without a thought in her mind—not even later, when she tried to reconstruct the scene—she whirled on the man and kicked him in the groin.

For two seconds—long enough for her to get back into the vestibule—the man let go.

"Mercy! Come quick!" Minna yelled and slammed the door.

From the porch, there was a howl.

Mercy came running.

The man's hand—or part of it—was caught between the door and the jamb.

"Push!" Minna yelled.

"We'll break the glass," said Mercy.

"Push!" Minna yelled again. "To hell with the glass. Just push ...!"

On the porch, the howling continued.

"You bastard!" Minna screamed. "Fuck off!"

Together, she and Mercy gave a final heave.

The door slammed. *Bam!*

Minna fumbled for the chain, found it and forced it into place. She also shot the bolt and turned the lock.

"I'm phoning the police," she said. "You watch and see which way he runs."

"He isn't running," said Mercy. "He's fallen to his knees."

Minna did not hear this. She was in the kitchen, dialling for help.

9

"Why are you stopping?" Col asked.

Bragg was parking the car in a laneway near Yonge and Dundas.

"Because," he said, "it's too early to go home."

"What are we going to do, then? *Sit* here?"

"No. We'll go to a bar and have a drink or two."

"Bragg—I can't just walk into a bar like this," Col said. "I'm wearing lipstick and high-heeled shoes."

"That's all right," said Bragg. "It's Hallowe'en! Come as you are! I'm going like this."

"You bugger." Col laughed. "Is this your revenge?"

"Revenge? What for?"

"For having to go to that dreadful party because I asked you to."

Bragg paused. Then he said: "here," and handed Col his handkerchief. "Use this. Remove the lipstick. I'll get those rubber boots we always keep in the trunk and you can throw the shoes in the back seat."

Walking into the bar at the Fairclough Hotel, Col remembered just in time to remove the pearl-drop earring. "Thank God for that," he muttered as they sat down.

Minutes later, having noted that ten men and the waitress were all staring at him, Col asked whether he had been successful in getting rid of the lipstick.

Bragg gave a smile.

"Yes," he said. "All gone. It's just ..."

"Oh, God—what?"

"Your lashes are falling off. And your mascara is running."

10

"Is he still there?"

"No. He's gone."

"Which way?"

"Towards the park."

"They'll find him."

Mercy did not sit down. She stood in the middle of the living-room and Minna thought she looked as if she was going to faint.

"You all right?"

"Yes." And then: "no."

"What is it?"

"We ... We ..."

"What? We what?"

"We've done something terrible."

"What? Because I kicked a rapist in the balls? Come off it."

"No," said Mercy. "No. Not that. It's ... this."

Mercy held out her hand, palm up.

Lying there was something black and torn—a fragment of Hell's Angel's glove—his gauntlet.

"So?" said Minna.

Mercy said: "there's a finger inside."

Minna said nothing

Then she said: "give it to me. Don't watch."

Mercy tipped the finger in its leather condom into Minna's hand and turned away.

Minna threw the finger into the fire.

"Done," she said. "It's over."

11

Bragg said: "Col?"

"Yes?"

"Are we happy?"

"Who's happy?"

"But—are we? Is it possible?"

"Sure it's possible."

"Even in spite of Minna?"

"I don't even know what that means, Stuart. Minna is the centre of both our lives."

"*You* love her, too?" Bragg said. "I'm astounded."

"No. I don't love her. But you do."

"Sometimes."

"No. Not sometimes. Always. You just said so."

"Did I? When?"

"You *love her, too?* you said. Positive proof that *you* do."

"But do you? How?"

"It's not love, Bragg. Not when you don't love women. Not what you mean by love—and not the *whammo* kind of love that we have. But I know who she is. She knows who I am. *Come as you are*, you said. We have no secrets, me and Minna. Not having secrets is a kind of love."

Bragg nursed his drink—a dreadful North American vintage— Beaujolais in name only.

"What will happen to us? Your version," he said.

Col sat back. He had peeled away Minna's lashes and—in the men's room—had wiped the streaks of mascara from his cheeks. He looked—but not completely—*normal.* His beauty, though male, was not masculine. His eyes were too far apart, too large for that—and his lips too sensual.

Masculine had straight, hard lines. Col's were curvaceous, wet and inviting. Masculine meant iron thin lips; eyes that said *no*; the fingers that were always curled, decisively rejecting any contact with *male* persons—any flesh that smelled of locker-room and sweat. *Don't, I won't let you—and sure as hell, I won't let me* was the message of everything learned about masculinity. *You can't come in—I won't come out.* It was the credo. Even women suffered because of it. *I can't,* masculinity said. *I won't.* That was the message.

Undo, women said. *Uncurl. Unfurl. Lie back. Expose yourself. You—it's you I want, not who you think you are. I want you—the person lying whole and naked on the bed.*

Bragg did not know this. Colin Marsh did. So did Minna. This was the war.

"Can we go home now?" Col asked.

"No," Bragg said. "She hasn't finished putting us aside."

12

"We just burned human flesh," said Mercy.

"That's right. One whole finger."

"This is not something people do."

"You think not?"

"Know not."

"He might have killed us," Minna said.

"Yes. But so what?"

"I beg your pardon?"

"Yes, but so what?"

"Yes—*but so what?*"

It lay there between them, like the finger on the vestibule tiles. Like the finger in Mercy's hand. The finger in the fire.

"He might have killed us," Minna repeated.

Mercy took off her hat.

"He can't kill me," she said. "I'm already dead."

She was completely bald.

Chemo.

Cancer.

Minna burst into tears.

13

When Col and Bragg returned at last, it was ten-fifteen. The police were there.

"Do these men live here?" one of the officers said.

"Yes," said Minna. "We have a *ménage à quatre.*"

"Pardon?"

"Nothing. Just a joke. This is my husband. That's his friend."

"Why police?" Bragg asked.

Minna told him.

"Jesus," said Bragg. "Are you all right?"

"I guess," said Minna. "I am—but the new dress ain't." She showed him. She did not explain the finger. Nothing was said about Mercy's impending death. "Sure," said Minna. "Yes. We're fine."

The policemen left.

In the morning, they would return. Hell's Angel would be captured—caught and held. Mercy would never forget him. Neither would Minna—for different reasons. Somewhere, deeply aside from where she spoke aloud, she would say to herself: *in my mind, for ... how long? One second only? For that moment, I thought:* if you let him in, you could be pregnant.

A rapist's child?

No. Not ever. Never.

Bragg's child only. Only Bragg's.

14

In her bed that night, alone, Minna thought: *Mercy will die and I will live. No children there—not one between us.*

Surely, good Mrs Murphy—Spud—will follow us all the days of our lives.

Tears ...

... in my ears as I lie on my back in my bed while I cry over you ...

Finger.

The bed was huge. Whenever Bragg was not there, it grew—or so it seemed. Six feet wide, to a football field. *Touchdown!*

No.

Field goal?

No.

Thirty yards? Forty?

Nothing.

Minna lay there—drifting.

The men had come home as from the hunt.

Empty-handed. Morose.

Mercy was dying. Dead. Cremated.

Finger.

Children came in droves to the door—*may I? Will you? thank you.*

Also—*fuck you.*

Angel from hell.

Wear my earring—shoes—mascara ...

Thank you.

Lipstick.

Someone. Someone. A baby. Somewhere ...

Mercy? Never. What she said—what? What was it? *Who needs another orphan?*

Dying. Dead. A finger. Cremated.

And ..?

And so ..?

Drift, now. Drifting.

Hold up your hands and lock your fingers ...

Minna—in her mindscape—made the gesture. All around, the sound of wind.

> *Here is the church,*
> *Here is the steeple;*
> *Open the doors, and*
> *Here are the people.*

Here are the people.

Drifting.

The steeple became a chimney. Down the chimney, someone fell. Not Santa Claus.

Alma.

Hello, Alma.

Hello, Minna.

Long time no see.

True.

I miss you.

Yes. And I miss you. All the dead miss all the living.
All the living miss all the dead.
Also, the unborn.
I beg your pardon?
What you mean is, all the living miss the unborn.
There was a silence—not quite total. Wind. The wind.
Minna sighed.
Soot. You're covered with soot.
That's what chimneys are for, Min. Soot. Delivery. Memory. Remembrance.
Soot. Delivery. Remembrance.
You okay?
Could be better—but—yes.
Wind. Alma began to fade—was fading.
See you, Minna.
No. Don't. Alma ...?
See you.
Going. Gone.
Bye now.
Yes. Goodbye.
Goodbye.
Minna slept.
The moon shone.
Starlight.
Thursday.

Hilton Agonistes

THIS IS WHAT HAPPENED.

By eight-fifteen, most of the guests were already drinking in the bars or seated in the dining-rooms. Out on the approaches beyond the bridges, the last of a horde of limousines was making its way to the hotel courtyard where, like all the rest, it would park and wait until its passengers had dined. In the tropical twilight, its headlamps had the look of messengers bringing the news that, in spite of the encroaching darkness, all would be well.

Down by the marina, three mahogany motor-launches, purring like baritone cats, sidled up to the docks and fell silent. Laughter was heard, and callings—names and greetings; someone distinctly saying: *isn't it wonderful! Isn't it fabulous!* A landing party of pale-skinned women and sunburned men began to make its way upward and along the paths—the women all in evening gowns, the men, as though in uniform, all wearing dinner jackets white as moonlight. These were the voyagers whose private yachts were anchored in the bay. A dozen or more came over every evening—one week the guests of Greek tycoons, the next of drug lords, deposed dictators, Hollywood film stars. Anyone. Almost.

In the tropics, darkness falls in the blink of an eye. *There goes the sun!* And with it, every trace of daylight. Nothing lingers. Gone. Shadows that seconds before had been delineated by the sinking sun leap to the moon's delineation, shifting before your eyes—now here, now there—in one swift movement.

On the path from the marina, lamps had been timed to come on automatically as darkness fell. *I feel as if we're in that scene from* Madame Butterfly, a woman said. *The one where all the lanterns flicker down the hill.*

Eight-twenty-five.

Nicholas Halifax, a middle-aged Canadian on holiday with his wife, Nicole, was still upstairs in the bedroom of their suite. His jacket lay on the bed, waiting for his attention. Nicole was seated, finishing her make-up. *Don't I look terrific,* she said. *Yes,* said Nicholas—not even turning. He was smoking a cigarette and sipping from a glass of gin and lime.

At home, where Nicholas had made a fortune selling bathroom fixtures, they were known—with some affection—as *The Nicks.*

Everyone is invited to The Nicks' for drinks—and everyone came. *We're celebrating our this—our that—whatever. Bring all your friends!* And everyone came with all their friends.

Two children, Francis and Maryanne, were being escaped. Francis, Maryanne, bathtubs, toilets, sinks and bidets. *Gone, for two whole weeks! How lovely, just for this little while, to be ourselves alone. A person deserves some peace from time to time. Isn't that true, Nicky?*

Yes, dear. Still not turning.

Out in the sumptuous darkness, the Georgian bridges with their rampant lions at either end were lit with lamps that had been made in Bristol.

The Queenstown Hilton sat on what had once been the site of the Governor's residence, parts of which now served as playrooms and gyms and spas for the guests. In the *Bad-Time-Before*—as the period was called—the mansion itself had been razed to the ground and not a trace remained. But its servants' quarters, stables and carriage mews had been saved.

The hotel grounds had always been a parkland, surrounded on every side by water—the residence sitting up on the heights with views in all directions. Iron fences had been installed—and gates. Also two cannon, each one trained on one of the bridges—the bridges sitting side by side, one for arrival, one for departure. Both cannons still there.

Beyond the bridges, the streets of Queenstown converged on a market square, where Nelson had a monument. In his younger years, the great man's ship had taken on provisions there and one of the island's famous mulattos had been his mistress—Bella Corteza, who had no monument.

The buildings of Queenstown were eighteenth century, mostly. One of the churches, built by the Spaniards, had been erected in 1548. The islanders themselves, once slaves, made up almost ninety per cent of the population. The dominant money, however, remained entirely white. *We pay, you do,* was how it was put—with a smile. And a hand withdrawn.

The *Bad-Time-Before* had occurred in 1865, as a result of

Lincoln's having freed the American slaves. Taking this symbolic moment to heart, the ex-slaves of Queenstown had determined they would renew their own freedom. Being "freed" in a British colony, after all, had meant nothing. Everyone had remained in place. The only difference was, you got paid for being a slave. The Governor and his wife were murdered—hacked to pieces on their lawn—and the garrison all but decimated. One week after the uprising, ships had arrived with hundreds of troops, and order had been restored—*order* having a uniquely white interpretation.

Now, there was more oppression than ever. The black population lived in thrall of white money. All the shops and restaurants in Queenstown were owned exclusively by whites, and patronized mostly by the wealthy tourists ensconced at the Hilton. A dozen sugar barons, living on the crests of hills, made up the entire population of rural employers. Every acre of countryside was under siege to sugar.

Drugs and prostitution were rampant. Men and women, boys and girls all made themselves available. If white, a person could not lie on the sand or walk in the street without being propositioned. Even Nicholas, balding and plain, had been offered *blow-jobs, ganja and girls.* In his lonely heart, a part of him had wanted to say *yes.* But his inbred sense of propriety had been outraged. *How dare these niggers say that to me!* In former, pre-proposition days, the words *blow-job* and *nigger* had never crossed his mind, let alone his lips.

Nicole had been sympathetic. *It's because you look so utterly American, darling. In your blue seersucker jacket and your tan Bermuda shorts, who would ever know you were Canadian? They*

*don't understand. We like black people—and we have no prejudice.
The problem lies in their accepting the easy way out. I mean, can you
imagine, Nicky darling, me on my knees before some unzipped poten-
tate just because I was poor!*

Of course not.

Nothing more was said on the subject. They still had one week
to go of their Hilton holiday.

Now, it was ten to nine.

Nicholas said: "there are lights out there."

"Lights?"

"Something—I don't know. Torches?"

Nicole stood up. She removed her plastic bib and smoothed the
front of her dress.

"Maybe there's a festival," she said.

"Maybe."

She crossed the room and stood beside him.

"Isn't it lovely? All that firelight ..."

"Torches."

"Yes. Torches are what they use, because they have to. Their
homes aren't lit, you know."

"You know that? How?"

"I talk to people. The gardeners. The maids. And one of
them—I think her name is Rose—told me her granny's house
burned down because a lamp was spilled."

"Spilled?"

"Yes. Kerosene."

"People live in houses lit by kerosene?"

"Of course. Why not?"

Nicholas gave his wife a look of incredulity. Nicole could not read it.

"*My candle burns at both ends,*" she said—and smiled. "*It will not last the night. But, ah, my foes, and, oh, my friends—it gives a lovely light.*" Still with her smile in place, she kissed him—open-mouthed. "Surely somewhere," she said, "there are people on this earth who think we must be barbaric, lighting our homes with lightning ..."

"You think so, do you?"

"Well—I wouldn't wonder."

For a moment, they were silent, watching the torch-bearers. Then Nicole said: "there isn't any music, which means—I guess—that it's not a festival."

"Perhaps it's political."

"But they're so quiet. I mean, if it was political, wouldn't somebody be making a speech?"

"Maybe they are, and we just can't hear it."

"It could be some sort of anniversary. You know? A vigil in someone's memory. That's why they're being so quiet. I mean—they're all in Nelson Square—do you think it's the anniversary of his death?"

Nicholas gave her a look that would have informed her, if she had seen it, that he thought her last suggestion too stupid for comment.

"I think we should go down to supper," he said. "All those flickering torches are beginning to make me dizzy."

He went across the room for his jacket, stubbing out his cigarette and setting down his glass on the way. He looked in the mirror and gave what remained of his hair another lick with the brush.

"Nicky?"

"Yes?" He was slipping into his jacket, settling its shoulders, pulling at its cuffs.

"I think something's happening."

"Oh? What?"

"I don't know—but come and look."

Nicholas crossed to the other window and pulled its curtains aside.

"Where?"

"In the square. The torches have begun to assemble in what look like columns."

It was true. The torches were lining up in pairs.

Someone started blowing a whistle. Then someone else—and someone else.

"They're heading for the bridges."

"Yes."

"Good heavens, Nicky. They're coming here."

"So I see."

"But why? *Why?*"

"I don't know." Nicholas's voice had lowered and was almost inaudible.

"What? What is it?" Nicole now sounded like a plaintive child, bewildered by some inexplicable force of nature—a rising wind, a darkening sky, a tidal wave.

Below them, in the ballroom, an orchestra had begun to play. Its music, typically, had an island flavour of calypso.

"Shall we go down and see?" Nicole asked.

"No. I think not."

"Why? Shouldn't we find out?"

"We can find out from here."

Nicholas went and poured more gin into his glass and drank it. Then he poured more and went back to his window.

"Aren't you going to give me one?"

"Fix it yourself."

"There's no need to snap at me."

Nicole went to the drinks table and filled a glass with gin and tonic water. "I wish we had more limes," she said. "You've used them all."

Nicholas said nothing. He was worried—baffled, but not yet afraid. What were they doing out there, blowing their whistles and making for the bridges?

Nicole was having a sequence of thoughts she knew were quite ridiculous. Saying nothing, she was conjuring explanations straight out of lunacy. *They're going to demonstrate some new dance on the lawn.* And: *they're going to sing a serenade to all the guests.* And: *we'll be invited to join them for some local celebration. Bonfires will be lit and ...*

She closed her eyes. And opened them.

The first of the torch-bearers had now reached the far side of the bridges. People stood up on the lions' heads and waved the others on. There were men and there were women.

"Oh," said Nicole. "Oh, Nicky."

Nicholas crossed the floor and went into the sitting-room.

"What are you doing?"

"I'm locking the door."

She heard him do this and, glancing over her shoulder, saw that he was also turning out the lights. When he returned, he closed and locked the bedroom door and pocketed the key.

Nicole watched him make his way from lamp to lamp.

"Must you turn out all the lights? I hate the dark."

"Tough."

In spite of his rudeness, Nicole said nothing. She was too concerned about the people on the bridge.

"They're angry," she said. She could see them clearly now, those who were already on the drive.

"Of course they're angry. That's what mobs are about."

"But why? And why come here? We haven't done anything."

"We are white, Nicole. We are North Americans. We are wealthy. We are staying at the god-damn Queenstown Hilton Hotel! We are everything they are not and we are *why* they are not!"

"Do you mean they're going to harm us?"

"No. I mean they are going to kill us. If they can. Oh, Jesus Christ! I cannot believe I didn't bring a gun!"

"Why would you bring a gun, Nicky? We're on our holidays."

"Yes. That's right. How could I have forgotten? We're on our holidays." He took a drink. "Christ!"

"Why are you angry with me?"

"For the same fucking reason they are. Because you're so god-damned fucking stupid!"

"Don't shout. They'll hear you."

The whistle-blowing had stopped. In the courtyard, on the lawns, the torch-bearers were silently surrounding the hotel.

The orchestra was still playing. *This is my island in the sun ...*

It was now nine-twenty-five.

In less than one hour, it would all be over.

The drivers of the limousines had stripped off their jackets and thrown down their caps. In the dining-rooms, all the waiters and waitresses had slipped away, and the kitchens had fallen silent, except for the hiss of steamers on the stoves.

Somebody said: "the angel of death must just have passed."

"Why?"

"Haven't you ever heard that? Whenever a silence descends in a crowded room—when all the occupants, for whatever reason, stop talking at the same time—that means the angel of death is passing over."

"Well, we've broken the silence, now, so everything must be all right."

It wasn't.

The doorways filled with figures.

The diners, seated, turned to gaze at them.

"Yes?" someone said. "Can we help you?"

There was no reply.

A machete was raised.

A whistle was blown.

Silent in their bedroom, Nicholas and Nicole remained apart—she in the chair where moments before she had gazed at her reflection in the mirror. *Don't I look terrific.* The image before her now was of a moonlit ghost—a woman so pale and insubstantial that she seemed to be underwater.

Nicholas stood with his back to the window, watching the door. Beneath them, the dining-room had become an abattoir and the sounds of slaughter might have been made by animals.

Nicole put her hands over her ears and shook her head from side to side as if the noise could be shaken free, like a cloak that had fallen over her. A cloak of screams.

Ten minutes. Twenty minutes. Half an hour of killing. At last, Nicole began to scream. "Make it stop! Make it stop! Make it stop!" She ran to Nicholas and beat at him with her fists. "I want it to stop! Oh, please, God, make it stop!"

She then began to sob and Nicholas led her over to the bed. For a moment, he sat beside her, one arm around her shoulders, patting her gently—soothing—attempting to soothe her.

"Soo-soo-soo," he said. "There, there, there."

When she was quiet, he got up and crossed the room, where he refilled their glasses.

"We mustn't speak," he said. "They may come looking for more."

Nicole accepted the drink, saying nothing. She was numb.

Nicholas went to the window and held his watch in the moon-light. Not quite ten-thirty.

An alarming silence had begun to manifest itself as the sounds from below died away. The air began to refill with insect noise, frog songs and bird calls. Nicholas even imagined he could hear the ocean. He stepped away from the window and lighted a cigarette.

In the hallway, beyond the sitting-room, people were moving—walking barefooted, he imagined—almost silent—only the whispering footsteps of someone either in pursuit or being pursued. The hunters and the hunted.

Nicholas went and stood beside Nicole. She bowed her head and took his sleeve in her hand.

A bell rang—the clock tower in Nelson Square. *Its song is so melodious,* Nicholas thought. When it was over, he took a deep breath and sighed.

In the evening quiet, they could hear someone come to the hallway door and try the handle.

Nicole's grip loosened on Nicholas's sleeve. Releasing him, she put her hand in her mouth.

Whoever it was tried the handle one more time and then again. Each time, there was the muffled sound of something metallic, jangling. Keys?

Don't.

And then, a most curious sound was heard: someone gently knocking at the door.

Nicholas froze.

Don't.

"Please," said a voice. "Is there anyone there?"

No.

The knocking was repeated.

Don't.

They waited. One minute. Two minutes. Three.

Someone was leaving. Departing. Their footsteps hissed down the corridor all the way to silence.

Oh.

Say nothing. Do not speak.

Nicholas's cigarette was burning towards his fingers.

He tiptoed back to the table and put it out in the ashtray. Then, with his drink, he returned to the window, stepping back from the moonlight—looking down at the courtyard.

They were leaving.

Men and women, exhausted, their shoulders drooping, their steps plodding, were walking down the drive towards the bridges. From their hands, machetes and unlit torches were dragged through the gravel.

It was over.

Nicholas turned around and looked at Nicole. Moonlit, she was weeping without a sound.

In the morning, they left the suite, still wearing their evening clothes. Just down the hall, they came to the first body. A woman in an orange robe. She was sprawled, face down, outside one of the doors.

Nicole leaned against the far wall and stared in horror as Nicholas knelt down and gently turned the figure over. One rigid arm struck the carpet. There was the sound of bracelets, jangling.

Not keys. Bracelets.

Oh. Don't.

Nicholas stood up, gazing down at what remained of the woman's battered face. He turned to Nicole and said: "close your eyes. I will lead you." And he took her hand.

"Where are we going?"

"Outside."

He led her beyond the elevator and down the stairs—past a dozen other bodies.

They finally reached the main floor. "Jesus Christ!" Nicholas muttered. "Don't look. Keep your eyes shut. Tight."

The doors of the great entrance were open, letting in a breeze.

He told her when they came to the steps and she hobbled down like a child, one tentative step at a time. At the bottom, they turned to the right and made for the gardens, Nicholas praying there would be no bodies there.

"I think we had best go down to the sea," he said. There were indications of mayhem in the flowerbeds beneath the dining-room windows. A human hand. An upturned face. Most of the windows had been shattered.

At the shore, where all was well, Nicholas told Nicole she could open her eyes.

Three mahogany motor-launches slapped at the water's edge and the wharf had sunlight on it. A day like any other day.

At the end of the dock, they turned and gazed back up at the hotel.

Its white walls were traced here and there with vines of bougainvillaea. Its broken windows stared as if in shock—wide-eyed and mad—at the sea. No one—nothing—moved.

"But where shall we go?" said Nicole. "And what shall we do?"

"Nowhere. Nothing. We shall wait."

"But, Nicky ..."

"We shall wait, Nicole. And, sooner or later, someone—surely someone will come."

"Yes, dear," she said. And then: "but who?"

Nicholas had no answer for this.

And so—beside the water, in the sunlight, turning away from the grand hotel on the heights, they chose two canvas chairs and, setting them apart, they waited.

Americana

SUPPERTIME, JANUARY 12TH: a Monday. 1970.

On Second Avenue there is a window filled with army ponchos, boots and a surplus of flags with forty-eight stars. There is also a plastic palm tree, giving shade, and—propped against two coconuts—a tinted photograph of Curtis LeMay. Up above the store front, a large and gaily lit sign shows a neon comet—yellow, with a long white tail. If it rains, the comet hisses; if it snows, the neon crackles like friendly fire. *HALLEY'S AMERICANA. WE BUY AND SELL.*

On summer evenings, George Halley puts out trays of books and boxes of beads for beaded curtains, wash sets stuffed with feather flowers, and two or three barrels of sugar bowls and moustache-cups. These are all made up by a firm in Harris, Ohio—copies of the real thing, antiqued with veins of amber tea-stain. Then he puts on a boater hat made of straw and stands in his pale blue shirt near his open door, eating peanuts and drinking beer.

Some nights he gets a chair and is sitting there still at twelve o'clock, with only a single light bulb behind him in the store, while the music from the Bar Arcade next door blasts in and out as the drinking patrons come and go.

On winter evenings, Mister Halley closes the shop at 6:00 P.M. and locks the door and steps into the Arcade for a beer and hamburg supper—or perhaps a hot beef sandwich. He doesn't sell much, so he can't afford much. But his window is aglow with light and every one of his shadowed wares is lit with beckoning nostalgia.

Sometimes people stop, as if to warm their hands on other times and places where the flag has flown—and sometimes a voice will say: *those were the days, eh, Harry? Can't you just feel those boots and smell that rain?* Then laughter, friendly obscenities and quiet.

Mister Halley's window, in the yellow air of evening, is a lonely place to stand in winter. But this night someone apparently content to do so stands there staring in, with his back to the street. A man perhaps twenty-three years old, in uniform.

He coughs, without putting his fist to his face, and the cough makes a white balloon in the air and a mess of steam on the window. Mister Halley's grey and yellow cat strolls out behind the glass and sits beside a pair of boots and, as if to prove it is a cat, it slowly begins to wash its face and ears with long, wet strokes. Its eyes are closed and the liquid motion of its paw is like a wind-up, faultless toy, each stroke ranging from mouth to ear, to chops and back again.

The soldier watches, hands idly playing in his pockets, turning over change in one and, in the other, fingering the flesh beneath his cotton underwear.

Behind him a woman and a man pass by arm in arm and the woman says: *it's only one block more and then we're there.* The soldier watches them flickering in and out of the window-glass, the man in an overcoat and muskrat hat, the woman in imitation fur.

A jolt of beery air from the bar announces two boys in leather and jeans. Laughing and flushed, they are playfully beating each other with chains.

The soldier, watching his world of reflections, sees them see him and pause. A curious silence ensues, as if the traffic had stopped. Then one boy says: *I've never had a sojer.* And the other giggles like a girl.

Sojer, calls the first boy, doing up leather buttons and hauling at a long, silver zipper on his jacket. *Hey ... so–jer! Pssst.*

The soldier does not turn.

Guess he didn't hear yuh, says the second boy. *He's lookin' in that window awful hard.*

Maybe they got a naked broad in there, says the first—and the soldier sees the reflection of a move in his direction.

Jesus, he thinks, *don't let them come too close.*

The two boys stare from behind the soldier, into the window, one of them brushing his thick long hair back from his face.

It's only a cat and some old shoes, he says.

An' a bunch of flags, the other adds.

Yeah. Shit.

The cat begins to lick its shoulder.

Silence.

The reflections float to the end of Halley's window, huddling together, putting on their gloves, which have brass studs.

I sure am hungry, one says.

Suppertime, says the other. *Yeah!* Then he giggles.

There is a rattle of chains. Then a slurring noise. An intake of wetted breath passing over clenched teeth.

Jesus, I tell ya. Am I ever starved!

Why not just go ahead and ask him, Rog?

There is a pause. And then, with a new tone of menace—louder, but still not addressed directly to the listener: *anyone 'round here got some meat to feed to the li-ons?*

The cat, perhaps hearing, looks up.

Someone goes in next door. The music roars. Jim Morrison. "Light My Fire."

He's deaf, says the other.

Then the one who had spoken first—the one with all the zippers and a halo of baroque hair, steps past his friend and says: *I offered you a blow-job, sojer. Whadaya say? You like that?*

The soldier turns.

Oh god ....

What is it? says the other. *What?*

The cat, alarmed, retreats.

The two boys run, the chains on their boots like sleigh bells, sounding into the distance. Gone.

The soldier stares in past the window.

It seems so tropically warm in there—the ponchos hinting of Indo-Chinese monsoons, and the boots of jungle stench. Curtis LeMay's jaws are swollen with a rare disease.

The palm tree shades the memory of mud. The cat returns and lies down to sleep.

Two young women hurry by, leaving their voices behind. *Late,* says one. *You're always late.* They both wear high-heeled boots and psychedelic colours. One of them carries an oversized cloth bag— a peace sign painted on its side.

Look at that poor soldier, she says.

Yeah. But we're late.

Up above, the neon comet wheezes in the cold. Perhaps it is going to snow.

It does.

The flags seem so warm, all bunched up and piled like that, and so the soldier thinks: *I'll stand here just a moment longer.*

An old man pauses and coughs.

Snowing, he says, reflected and friendly.

Yes.

You on leave?

Oh yes.

You want some place to stay?

There is a pause. Then: *Mister?*

Yes, boy?

Fuck off.

Footsteps. Gone, with all the others.

The soldier is crying, now. *What is it,* he says to himself aloud, *that makes them want me so ...?*

One last person arrives at his side.

Hello, she says.

Hello.

You lookin' at the cat, kid?

Maybe.

Nice, eh? The cat.

It has a crick in its tail.

Does it? I don't see no crick.

The cat obligingly yawns and tucks its tail out of sight. It sleeps.

The woman wears an old cloth coat and a ratty scarf. Her hair needs brushing. On her feet, an undone pair of rubber galoshes.

I didn't see no crick, she says. *I think you must be pulling my leg. Maybe.*

You on leave?

No. Are you?

That's very funny. Shallow laughter. *I like a sense of humour.*

The cars on the street have begun to jam up. Horns are honking. The foggy air is yellow.

Listen, the woman says. *They won't let you go in half the bars if you look the way I do. Can you help me, soldier? Have you got a place to stay? I wouldn't even charge you. Honest. And I ain't gonna roll you—honest to Jesus I won't. But I have to get a place to stay—or else I freeze out here an' go to jail.*

No, says the soldier, *I'm only passing through.*

Okay. Okay. Shit on you, buster! Shit on you! I thought you looked like a guy who'd understand.

Leave me alone, the soldier says. *Fuck off.*

And so she does.

And now Mister Halley comes politely belching from the Bar Arcade, his arms full of beer and bagels. He steps towards his door.

Good evening, soldier. Happy New Year.

New Year's is over, says the soldier.

Oh, well, yes, says Mister Halley. *I guess it is.* Pause. *Say ...*

Mister Halley looks the soldier up and down.

Would you like to come in and have a beer?

The soldier sighs and says: *yes.* Finally. *Yes.*

They go inside to the palm-tree warmth—the flags, the boots and the cat.

Mister Halley dumps the beer and the bagels on a more or less empty tabletop and turns on some lights.

You like my window? he says. *I noticed you looking.*

Yes. It reminded me. A little.

Dare say. Yes. I dare say. You from the War?

A nod.

I thought so. Nam.

You Mister Halley?

That's it. Halley—as in comet.

The opening of beer. A guzzle.

I've been looking in your window. I've been thinking ...

Well, that's good. I guess we could do with more of that. Mister Halley laughs. *The flag is good. But ordinary. Doesn't get too many stares. The ponchos and the boots? I sell a few, but mostly ... can you manage? Your mouth? A glass? No. Well, mostly, I was going to say, we get—how to put it—(laughter)—rubber freaks—you know the kind? I change the General once a week. Last week I had MacArthur and two weeks back it was Patton. But people forget. You need a gimmick to sell. The only thing is to find one.*

The soldier fingers his can of beer as he speaks: *that's sort of what I been thinking about,* he says. *'Round here, there's sure a lot of buying and selling going on, Mister Halley.*

I think I know what you mean. Hookers of every 'suasion. (A wink.) *Have another?*

Thank you. Yeah. What you need is to get folks in to buy this army stuff. Right?

That's it. That's the ticket.

Well, Mister Halley—sir, I think I got the gimmick that'll do it.

How?

All the while I stood there, looking in your window, I must've been propositioned twenty times. You know? Hookers of every 'suasion?

So?

Do you think it was because I'm beautiful?

No. To be frank.

I've been there—where the window says, the soldier says. *In Nam. It's obvious.*

The soldier takes a long cool breath and gives his cough and waits. Then he says: *why don't you put me in the window?*

I don't understand.

It's the flesh and blood they want to buy, Mister Halley. The wounds.

The wounds?

Look.

The soldier, rising, opens and casts down all his clothes to the floor and stands there naked, his back to the window, before George Halley.

Mister Halley sucks his teeth. He does not speak.

For a weekly wage, the soldier says, *you may touch them.*

Mister Halley, gulping at his beer, sits still as placid water. But in the soldier's mind, he reaches out with his fat little fingers, his eyes aglow with pity.

You got yourself a deal, Mister Halley says. Out loud. And then: *is that a burn? What on god's earth did they do to you there? Stand closer, boy. Beneath the light.* He watches as the soldier turns from side to side. *Gracious. I never would've believed. Do they hurt?*

Of course they hurt, you fucking madman.

No, says the soldier. *I have no pain.*

He watches Halley's eyes, thinking of the leather queens, the destitute prostitute, the old man. He knows what's in Halley's mind. *May I put them in my mouth?*

Yes. You may lick them. That is what wounds are for. Other people's solace.

On Second Avenue there is a window filled with army ponchos, old boots and a surplus of flags with forty-eight stars. There is also a plastic palm tree, giving shade, and now, this week—a tinted photograph of "Phil" Sheridan, propped up against two coconuts. Beneath the photograph is that good General's slogan: *War is hell.*

On an army cot, on which it alternately sits and lies, is the figure of a semi-naked man, wearing tattered trousers and an undone jacket, displaying a range of wounds from head to toe that some have called perfection; matchless. Others, miraculous. And when the figure lies down to rest, a yellow and grey cat appears and slips into its lap and licks its wounds.

Always, a large crowd gathers outside to stare, and the leather queens come and go, and the rubber freaks and the old, old men and the pinch-waist prostitutes and the gentle, pretty ladies and the vacant, uniformed marines and ...

Up above the window is a large and gaily lit sign, decorated with a comet: ascendant. If it rains the comet hisses. If it is cold and snowing the neon crackles. Just like friendly fire.

"HALLEY'S AMERICANA. WE BUY AND SELL."

Infidelity

THE BENCH WAS the same. The fountain. The trees. There was a dog, the way there had been—open windows—someone listening to music. Also the terracotta planter full of red geraniums and blue lobelia sitting on its stone step.

The dog might have been the same. I could not remember. But the same intent had brought him to this place. A rendezvous with scent.

I sat on the bench and closed my eyes, wondering if the voices would begin again.

When I first went up through the village streets to this little park with its trees and bench and fountain, I had been looking for somewhere to smoke a cigarette. I needed somewhere off the beaten track, where I could be fairly certain Mary, my wife, would not find me. I hadn't smoked in over a year and my work, as a consequence, had not gone well. I couldn't articulate a single thought on the page. I couldn't sit in my chair—I couldn't look at the blank sheets of paper without a sense of hopelessness. I was endlessly fidgeting with different pens—spending whole days gazing at all the familiar objects gathered there to spur me on—including the glazed green ashtray Mary had given me. *This is for the butt-ends of your days.* Then, a year ago, I had decided there was nothing for it but to surrender. If I wanted the breakthrough I needed in order to meet a deadline, I was going to have to start smoking again.

It would break Mary's heart. And anger her. This was implicit. *If I gave it up, so can you*, she had said. This was true. If I smoked two packs a day—which I did—Mary had smoked three. She had lived inside a wavering cloud that drifted after her and settled over her whenever she walked across a room and sat down. Except when she slept and ate, there had not been a moment without there being a cigarette in her hand.

I am a writer. Mary is a painter. Both activities require intense concentration. When she first tried to work without cigarettes, it was murder. When I first tried—it was hell on wheels. State the difference. You can't.

Sadly, our marriage took a beating during that time. It was as if the cigarettes had been what kept us together and, once they were gone, we fought the way other couples do when something irrevocable has caused them pain—each one berating the other until there is nothing left of trust. We spent whole hours together, sullen and silent. We started not sleeping in the same room. There was a lot of door-slamming and terse complaining: *must you scrape your plate like that?* and *why can't you learn how to park a car?* Always said in the presence of others—others increasingly turning down our invitations, awkwardly finding excuses not to stand beside us at cocktail parties. We had become unpopular—each with the other—both, in the world at large. All because we had given up smoking.

Now, once more, we were back in France, where we spent three months of each year in a rented house. Luckily for us, the owners of the house preferred to summer in England, where they had extensive gardens best enjoyed while the days were at their longest. Consequently, for over six years we had been coming to the village of Carmignac in the Var, arriving on the first day of June and departing on the last day of August. There was only one drawback to this scheme. It meant we missed the best months at home in Canada. Still, it was worth it. Or had been, up until last year. That was when I started smoking again.

I can still remember standing outside the Bar Tabac, wondering if I was really prepared to enter. Of course, in my heart of hearts, I knew I was going to, but I wanted to put up some kind of fight so I could say: *at least I tried.* This indecision lasted about five minutes—and ten minutes later I was walking past the *boulangerie* and the church in search of a convenient backwater. I found it beyond an archway that rose between two houses, bridging over a narrow *ruelle* that led yet further upward over some cobbled steps into the sunlight. A *ruelle* is a kind of streetlet. A narrow lane between houses. I took the turning and, once the sunlight had been achieved, I found myself in a miniature Eden.

A fountain spilled its water into a basin made of stone and, from that basin, down to another where dogs could drink. A single bench, unoccupied, sat against a wall, and over all of this, three albizzia trees spread their dappled shade. It was utterly charming—beguiling and perfect. There was even a refuse container sitting in the corner, waiting for me to deposit the cellophane wrapping from my box of cigarettes. Blue. *Fine 120. Super length. Légères.*

I sat down and struck a match. I watched it burn—and then I struck another. *Well, here goes ...*

The effect was unexpected. almost alarming. After the first and second puffs, I had to lean forward, my head between my knees. I thought I was going to faint.

I had forgotten this—the sudden loss of oxygen and what it does to the brain. If people had passed along the *ruelle* in that moment, I'm sure they would have thought I was hopelessly drunk—or stoned. I might as well have been. For about three minutes, I could not stand up. I couldn't even sit back. I hung there, helpless as someone coming out of an anaesthetic haze.

That was when the dog arrived and began to drink from the fountain. Normally, I would have spoken to it—*bonjour, chien*—but I couldn't even do that. Speak? Forget it.

While the dog was drinking, I forced myself into an upright position. Beyond one of the open windows off to my left, a woman was having a telephone conversation.

"*Oui. Oui. D'accord,*" I heard. "*Oui. Oui. La même chose.*" There was a pause—and then: "*non! Pas possible! Oh, mon Dieu. Oui. Oui. Oui ... Non! Oui? Oh, mon Dieu ... Ah, oui. Je comprends. Oui. Moins nous parlerons mieux cela vaudra, oui? Oui. D'accord. Merci, Jeanne. Merci. Non, non, non—jamais. Rien. Oui. A tout à l'heure.*" CLICK.

A scandal. But what?

Moins nous parlerons mieux cela vaudra, oui? The less said the better ... although it seemed to me a very great deal had been said. The trouble was, it had all been said at the other end of the line.

What a pity I hadn't been able to hear Madame Jeanne's contribution to the conversation—the part where she spilled the beans—or perhaps, from the sound of it, placed a few knives.

I took a longer draught of smoke and savoured it. The feeling I had longed for was beginning to come—the feeling, ironically enough, that I could breathe again. And think. And formulate. And plot. And articulate. God—it was sinister. That something so destructive should be so productive at the same time. *While I kill you, I will give you a few good ideas, n'est-ce pas?* Damn it all, it was insidious.

The dog was lying in the shade, ignoring my presence entirely. I might as well have been a figure carved in stone, for all the interest he took in me. Perhaps there was always someone sitting on that bench when he came for his drink and his bit of shade. He was an old dog—thin and worn and worldly wise. Black—with a shiny white ruff and two white paws. Clean and—I was glad to see—wearing a collar. He was not an abandoned dog—not a homeless dog. Just independent. No infidelity there. Not running riot with a gang of others, chasing sheep in the valley. Not off smoking behind his wife's back. Not causing scandal along the phone lines. Just lying down beside the fountain, cool on the grass beneath the albizzia trees, watching a neighbourhood cat as she washed herself in the sunlight.

Oh, I thought, *if only we could all be so relaxed and at peace with ourselves.* Dogs don't smoke. Cats don't. They go about their business with animal efficiency and never regret for a moment the absence of some alien substance that promises to save their sanity.

Another voice obtruded—this time, speaking English.

Whereas the first voice had emerged from one of the courtyard houses gathered around my park, this voice was coming from somewhere out of sight around the corner. To my right, the *ruelle* rose in two directions, each arm disappearing into a maze of houses—all the houses with open windows, spilling lace curtains into the air and sporting window boxes filled with geraniums, marigolds, impatiens.

"Hello—it's me. Yes."

Another woman.

I was startled by the accent. I thought I knew all the Americans in Carmignac—but none of them lived up here. Who could this be? It was a pleasant voice—but tense.

"He's in the bathroom, now," the woman was saying. "He'll be leaving as soon as we've said goodbye. Give me ten minutes. Fifteen. See you." *CLICK.*

More scandal. Even the dog had lifted his head to hear it. Perhaps he belonged to the woman we had overheard. Or to the man she was about to betray. If that, in fact, was what she was going to do. She might, after all, have been talking to a relative. She might have been talking to a friend, with whom she was planning some happy surprise for the man who was leaving home— and when he came back, a lobster dinner would be waiting for him. Or a set of new golf clubs.

But I knew better. The tone of the woman's voice told me that, and the inflection given to the words *give me ten minutes. Fifteen.* Time enough to hide the body? Put the fifty million francs she had stolen from him into a shopping bag? Burn the evidence? Evidence of what?

Infidelity.

It was a certainty. *He's in the bathroom now—give me ten minutes ...*

I waited for the toilet to flush. For taps to be run. For a man's voice saying: *I've decided not go to Paris.* Or wherever.

That was it. When he came around the corner and started down the *ruelle* towards the archway, I would whisper to him: *don't go.*

The cigarette had almost burned its way to the filter. And while it had done so, two other lives besides my own had been placed in jeopardy. No. Not lives—but their happiness—their surety. Madame Jeanne's anonymous victim had thought her secret was safe—that no one knew what she was up to. Now, the whole world knew. Certainly the whole village. And the man? Well—maybe he was leaving home on a business trip, during which he planned a little infidelity of his own. A little or a lot. How would one ever know? But, whatever he was up to, his wife—his lady friend—his mistress—his companion—whatever she was—was up to her own skulduggery.

The cat, who had finished her bath, was sleeping now on the stones. I dropped the butt-end of my cigarette to the sand at my feet and ground it out with my toe. Such a delicate, graceful gesture—the heel and ankle raised, the shoe—a loafer, glinting in the sun—the dancelike precision of the grinding. And the ugly mess it made ...

I retrieved the flattened filter—the torn paper—the compacted tobacco and carried them to the refuse container. Sitting back down, I heard a door being opened. And closed.

I got out another cigarette. Another match. The man was coming. I could hear him. I did not light up. I waited.

His footsteps had a ring of confidence to them—of energy—of certainty. His destination was already implicit in the way he was moving towards it. He also had no qualms about the situation he was leaving behind him—nor about the woman to whom he had just said goodbye. His step was absolutely debonair.

Give me ten minutes. Fifteen.

There he was. Dressed in a pale summer suit—its jacket swinging from side to side down his back, dangling there from the fingers of one hand raised to his shoulder. In the other hand, his expensive, soft leather bag. Brown. A weekend bag and, lying against it, a slim mahogany-coloured briefcase. He wore a yellow tie and a blue cotton shirt. He was pencil-thin, six feet tall or slightly more. Black, grizzled hair. Tanned—with sun-glasses hiding his eyes—a beaklike nose—very "French"—and a wide self-satisfied mouth. He was humming—something tuneless, just a sound to walk to. Almost a marching song.

Wait. Don't go ...

No. It was none of my business.

The dog sat up to watch him. The cat gave a stretch and set her chin against the stones beneath her, watching also, through hooded, half-open eyes.

All of this took ten, perhaps twelve seconds. The man was now below me, crossing the courtyard that served as a crossroads for the *ruelle* and a second alley that disappeared in either direction left to right. A boy—perhaps fifteen or less—came to the window through which the music could be heard. He was wearing nothing but a red towel and his hair was wet. I expected him to call down some sort of greeting to the man, whom he must have known. He didn't. He stood there oblivious of me—and equally uncaring about the figure now directly below him. Surely, since they were neighbours, something would be said. But, no—nothing. The man kept on walking. The boy went back inside his room and put on another tape.

I watched the man's back, with its swaying jacket, all the way to the bottom of the *ruelle*, where—stepping under the archway into the street—he turned towards the village *cours* and was gone.

I lighted the second cigarette—suddenly coming to and seeing it in one hand and the match in the other.

The dog went back to sleep. The cat had barely wakened. The music was played at a sensible level. The songs were rather pretty, sung by a woman whose voice I did not recognize. Romantic. Sentimental. Sad. All about lost or unrequited love. The boy would be getting dressed now, perhaps anticipating a rendezvous of his own. At that age, showers are taken only for two reasons: you have either just come off the playing field, or you have a date.

I wished I had looked at my watch when the woman had said: *give me ten minutes. Fifteen.* Now, I had no idea where the time-line was in her story. And she might, for all I knew, choose another direction when she left for her ... what? Her lover's arms? A weekend in the country? (It was Friday, after all.)

And, if I did see her, what would she look like? The man had been reasonably handsome. Thirty-eight, perhaps—or a healthy forty-two. It had been hard to tell. The woman might be the same age. Maybe younger. Money was involved somehow in their lives. The man's suit had been Italian—tailored—expensive. And his haircut had a monied look—the *salon* look of someone who spent whatever was needed to achieve the appearance he wanted. She, I assumed, would be the same—well turned out—and trim. And beautiful. She was, after all, the object of desire in two men's lives. At least two men.

Then—I heard her. Or presumably.

A door—the same, or another?—was opened and closed. And locked.

Locked.

This meant the house she was leaving had no other occupants. He, of course, was gone. There were, therefore, no children—no aged parents—no servants.

She was moving in my direction. Slowly. (That was odd.) She even stopped for a moment. Hesitant. Something had been left behind, perhaps—forgotten. She would go back. Or perhaps she had changed her mind. No rendezvous, after all.

I waited—barely able to deal with the suspense. Thank God for the cigarette. I was almost sick with apprehension. How had this happened? All I had done was overhear a short conversation—and I was already so embroiled in these people's lives I might just as well have been writing them.

Whatever had caused the woman's hesitation had resolved itself. Nothing forgotten—no need to go back. The rendezvous would proceed. And here she was.

No. It could not be her.

The man might conceivably have been her son. She was in her sixties—elegant, as he had been, though less carefree about it. She wore a soft wool suit, the colour of sand—its jacket buttoned up *à la chinoise*. Her hair, pure white, was brushed away from her forehead, giving the impression of wings. She carried a shoulder bag and her shoes had flat heels. She walked with purpose—but

without a sense of urgency. She had once been very beautiful—
and was handsome, still, though I could not see her eyes. She, too,
was wearing dark glasses.

Mothers, of course, have love affairs. In France, they have them
into great old age. And if the young man's father was still alive—
and still her husband—perhaps she had wanted not to offend her
son with her infidelity. This could be. And yet ...

I did not believe it. Perhaps because I preferred the story of a
more conventional affair—a middle-aged woman or a woman
approaching middle age who was having one last fling before
menopause. Mary would have laughed at my thinking that—but
I'm a man and there are things about women I will never understand. Comprehend, perhaps, but not understand.

The woman had now crossed over the courtyard and was passing beneath the boy's open window. Not looking up, she raised
her hand in greeting—or was it a signal? Either way, he was not
there to see it. Or to see her stepping sideways under the arch,
where—like the man before her—she turned to the right and
made for the *cours*.

What could have been in my mind, when I thought: *or was it a
signal?* The stories of these people's lives was getting out of hand.
They were now *conspirators*! A giant step beyond mere infidelity.

An older woman—a younger man—a boy ... It happens.

Good lord! Was the boy her lover?

Don't be ridiculous.

Except—it was not ridiculous. Improbable, perhaps, but not
ridiculous. I myself had a brief encounter with an older woman
when I was sixteen. Admittedly, she was not in her sixties. More

like twenty-five. But it lasted for three whole weeks one summer when I was a counsellor at camp and she was the cook. She had asked me to join her one night for a clandestine beer after we'd been for a swim in the lake. Once we were back in her cabin, she'd said: *it isn't healthy to sit around in wet bathing suits* ... And-what-do-you-know? She just happened not to have any towels handy. Of course, one thing led to another and, after that, we went swimming every night. Until her husband arrived. At which point, she said: *didn't I tell you, Charlie, about my husband?* Big oversight. And, come to think of it, my first involvement with infidelity.

I was remembering all this—sort of drifting into the past as a way of ridding my mind of *les affaires de ruelle*, when I heard a new set of footsteps.

Ten minutes. Maybe fifteen.

It was somewhere in between since the man had gone past.

The dog was curious. And so—to some degree—was the cat. They both looked up to see who might be coming. The step was louder—more assured than the older woman's had been. Feminine—but younger. There was a sort of *clip* to it—almost something of a dance. Or performance. The way an actress will make an entrance—radiant, with arms outstretched—coming expectantly down a staircase.

Stop that!

This is madness.

I turned on the bench.

Leave these people alone. They have lives to live. Let them.

But I could not help looking back. What if it was her? The wife—woman—mistress—companion. I had to know what she

looked like—and if it was her, if I decided absolutely it was her—
I would follow her.

I beg your pardon?

All right. No. I wouldn't follow.

But maybe. Depending.

She was black. I'd never seen anyone so beautiful. I must have
made a sound. She turned and saw me.

Yes?

I looked away. *I wasn't staring. Honest.*

She adjusted her gait and continued down the path.

Where the *ruelle* crossed the *rue* she stopped and turned her
head over her shoulder. *Me?* Or the boy with his music? The dog?
The cat?

She gave us all a look of farewell.

I am never coming back, it said. And she was gone.

I sat desolate. The man—the boy—the two women—each had
a story, but I would never know the outcome.

I was out of breath—somehow exhausted—the way you are
after an exhilarating meeting with someone whose absence leaves
you depleted. Adrenalin up—adrenalin down. Like that. And
now, someone else was coming.

I lighted my third and, I swore, my final cigarette.

Smoking is not only bad for your health. It is bad for other
people's privacy.

And here was the third of the candidates just coming into view.
Blonde—*of course*—with a pair of stylish sun-glasses riding in her
hair—and a thin, hungry mouth and blue, seditious eyes.

Seditious eyes is good, I thought. Use it.

Having rejected the first two women out of hand, I was determined this would be the one. Godlike, I was making up their lives on the spot.

The blonde was a perfect match for the tall dark man—small, compact, energized. She would look superb beside him. I could see him choosing her at a bazaar. *Would you ask her to stand just here ...?* he would say to the salesman. *Could she pull her hair back—not too far—like that—yes, yes. I'll take her ...*

Or, perhaps, the other way around. She had gone hunting for him—and found him trying on Spanish shoes—or choosing four Italian sweaters—or presenting his card at Penhaligon's in Covent Garden: *I'll have four bottles of the Blenheim Blend and six boxes of the fern soap ...* Or maybe dining at Goldoni's in Venice or drinking at the Dôme in Paris. Or ...

I watched her through slitted eyes.

She had paused, I was surprised to see, beside the cat, who was scratching her head. The cat, I was equally surprised to see, endured her attentions without unsheathing her claws or spitting cat-invectives in her face. I took a hefty drag of the cigarette and blew it in her direction.

This woman could not be French, I decided. It was not in her carriage—certainly not in the shape of her mouth. Yet the man, I was certain, must have been French—if not Italian. Or Spanish. Or ...

And why not? *The Jet-set jets.* That's the whole point. Thousands of wealthy Brazilians end up married to thousands of filthy-rich Australians and thousands of titled Brits end up married to thousands of Bostonian millionaires. Married, or something. Then they all move to Carmignac and start being unfaithful to one another. It happens every minute of every day.

Watching her scratch the cat, I thought: *you've taken him for every sou and now, the minute his back is turned, you're off to play bed-games with your lover boy.*

Yes. And you look just like Mary …

This hadn't occurred to me until she straightened to walk away from the cat. There was something in the way she lifted the back of her hand to her hair in order to push it farther away from her face—a gesture Mary made twenty times a day. Also something in the way she adjusted the shoulder-strap of her bag, settling it in between the bones—dropping her hand to the bag and moving on across the courtyard and down beneath the arch. Nothing for the boy. She obviously had no idea he was even there. His music had stopped.

Mary.

What had she been up to all this time I'd been away in my little park? Not *what had she been doing?* but *what had she been up to?*

Was this the day—was it on Fridays the *jardinier* came—that impossibly good-looking man who never wore a shirt? The one Mary had wanted to pose for her in the nude, but she'd never had the nerve to ask him. He was hired, after all, by the owners of the house, not by us, and he might make some kind of complaint and have us kicked out. *That would never do, would it,* she had said after a funny smile. Not *that would never do*—but *that would never do, would it.* The difference is subtle, I grant you—but there is a difference. If a person says *that would never do,* they mean it—period, end of story. But if they add *would it,* they mean to consider it as a possibility—if they can figure out a way to get away with it.

Get away with it.

There you are, then.

Now, I was in a total panic. God! How long had I been gone? Hours? I'd told her I was taking my lunch in the *cours*, which I did before I bought the cigarettes. We rarely ate together at noon. We worked at different times of day. I looked at my watch. It was only just after three. I had left the house at noon. And walked into the village. Wouldn't you know it? Now, I'd have to walk back. If only I'd brought the car, I would get there in five minutes, park under the trees across the road where she couldn't hear me arrive. then I could sneak around to the side of the house and look through the windows.

Yes—and there he'd be. Starkers. Probably smiling. Well-made men always do when you look at them naked. *Now you know why I'm famous!*

Hah!

She'd never asked me to pose for her in the nude. Not that I would have, of course—but a person likes to be asked. The fact is, I'm not all that great looking—even with clothes on. But, dammit, a person's wife could lie about it. Just to bolster a man's pride. And so forth.

And so on.

Oh, God. She's having an affair with the gardener—and all I did was sneak a couple of cigarettes.

Three.

I stood up and threw the final butt in the refuse can and started walking away. I would go home and tell her I had started smoking again and then I would inspect her sketch-pads. Or I would just simply say: *Mary—I'm smoking again. Are you having an affair?*

Stepping away from the grass, I turned over my shoulder. One must not forget one's companions ...

"*Au revoir, chien. Bonne journée.*"

And then: "*et vous aussi, minou,*" to the cat.

I wanted to yell up at the boy, who remained invisible: *stop right now, before you ruin your whole bloody life!* But I was too late. In the very moment I spoke to him in my mind, he appeared in the courtyard, hair hanging down suggestively over one eye, a torso-hugging shirt and an air of practised nonchalance. I let him pass me—catching, as I did, a whiff of his father's cologne. *Wear this for me and good hunting.*

After that, I marched like a one-man search-and-destroy unit through the *cours* and out of the village to our road.

Mary was sitting at the kitchen table with a glass of wine. Something was definitely wrong. She was tense and did not want to look at me.

"I have something to tell you," she said.

I bet you have! Where the hell is he?

"Oh, Charlie ..." Good Lord, she was actually crying.

"So," I said—attempting diffidence. "What is it? Tell me."

"I feel so bad. I've tried so hard."

"MARY! JUST TELL ME!" I shouted the whole line.

She bit her lip.

"I'm sorry," she said, "but I've started smoking again."

Saying this, she took a package of Gauloise from her pocket and laid it on the table.

I stared at it. One whole minute of silence later, I began to laugh. I laughed and laughed and laughed. What else could a person do?

———————

Afterwards—as they used to write in novels rife with infidelity—we lay on the bed and watched our smoke rising up towards the ceiling.

At last, I sat up and set my feet on the floor.

"Where are you going?" she said.

"I'm going to my desk," I told her. "And, if you want, you can come and sketch me. In the nude. It's such a lovely day, I'm going as is."

Which I did. And wrote this story.

The drawings, by the way, are spectacular.

The Madonna of the Cherry Trees

1

ANGELS AND ARCHANGELS—some with wings and some with swords. Virgins seated and Virgins standing. Baptists clasping lambs in broken arms. Jewelled Saints and flaming Martyrs. Every eye on heaven. Twice a week, the Vergerine sisters confronted this treasure-trove of pain and ecstasy—fell on their knees and polished the toes, swabbed the stigmata and buffed the fingernails.

They might have been nuns in a private order, Tuesdays and Thursdays, gliding in from the vestry, skating across the stones in mop-soled shoes, their pockets full of dusters. Maryse, Thérèse and tiny Babette—Babette known as "the shrimp"—*la crevette*—four-foot-five, with glasses thick as double glazing. Only she was able to skate behind the knees of the seated Christ of Aquitaine. *He has the nicest thighs*, she had said on the first occasion, prompting Thérèse to crawl in after her. There in the gloom, caressing those parts that only the sculptor's fingers and her sister's had explored before her, she released a sigh that was almost a moan of pleasure.

Nervous of the priests preparing for matins, Maryse had whispered hoarsely: *come out from there at once!*

Emerging still on her knees, Thérèse had sunk back onto her heels, biting the end of her duster reflectively. Babette had giggled. *Thérèse is in love with Jesus' legs.*

Thérèse had not replied. Rising to her feet, she had glided off towards the choir, gazing back with languid intensity at the figure of the seated Saviour. Clearly, the Christ of Aquitaine had taken on new meaning.

In their long grey smocks, black stockings and rag-bound hair, the Vergerine sisters were known to everyone. To watch them drift beneath the vaulted ceilings, caught in the early-morning light— here one, there another—skating between the pillars in their wide-mopped shoes, was to see some ancient ritual dance performed by ghosts. The stones beneath their feet shone in the wake of their passing, and every holy hand and cheek gave up its dust as if the poor had come to collect their alms. The sisters might have been retired, but none of them would hear of it. *No one knows this dust like we do*, Maryse—always the leader—would say, *and we mean to stay here till we're part of it.*

Each of them was relatively healthy, barring an ache or two. The dust had never bothered them. *Our lungs reject it*, Maryse had told Père Gérard, the priest in charge of their duties. *Twice a week, we get to polish His Majesty's toes*—His Majesty being Jesus Christ—*and surely you wouldn't deny us such a privilege.*

This way, in 1996, the Vergerine sisters remained as much a fixture of the great cathedral at Villeverger as its famous Madonna of the Cherry Trees, its Holbein altar screen and its choir stalls carved by the Master of Burgoyne. And, of course, its Christ of Aquitaine.

Villeverger, perched on its hill in the Hautes-Pyrénées, might seem an inconsequential site for such a prestigious cathedral, but that was the way of things in medieval times. A miracle had happened there and miracles must be commemorated. In 1348, at the height of the Black Death, the Virgin Mary had appeared among the cherry trees in the orchards which gave the town its name. According to some, she had carried the Christ child in her arms—and her presence there had saved the inhabitants from the pestilence and its ravages.

Pilgrims had arrived. Having lost his wife, the sainted Jeanne of Burgundy, to the plague, Philip II—King of France—had brought his court to pray beneath the trees where the Virgin had walked. Consequently, Philip himself and his son, the Dauphin, were spared. It was Philip's purse that paid for Villeverger's famous spires, though it would take another century for the whole cathedral to be completed. Now, it stands on its hill, the old town coiled about its steps and the new town, post-1945, spreading encroachment on the cherry fields—ten thousand trees whose ancestry cannot be calculated. The orchards there are walled with stones as old as Charlemagne.

2

In 1940, Maryse had met and married René Bouchard. She was seventeen—he was nineteen. Less than one month later, he was dead—among the slaughtered at L'Abbaye Frossart. He might have been a priest, she had decided, dying a martyr's death in a monastery far from home in the hills of Normandy east of Rouen. *René—l'adorable.* There had been no children. *They will come later. Later* never came. Maryse did not remarry. None of her sisters had taken husbands. They had reached the end of their line.

Born in the old town, they had never gone down to see the new. It depressed them—especially Maryse—with its squared-off houses and tawdry American advertisements: Quality Inns. McDonald's. Euro-Disney. *How have we come to this,* she complained to one and all, *whose choir stalls were carved by the Master of Burgoyne?*

The farthest the sisters had ever ventured had been to Vichy in the early forties. Everyone went there once at least in that time. Pétain must be seen to be believed: the hero of Verdun and now their leader. Standing hand in hand with her sisters, her father and her mother—Maryse almost fell to her knees when he passed in his motorcar.

Many times, until the consequences of the war destroyed her faith in him, she had compared the experience of seeing the Grand Marshall with the experience of those who had seen the Virgin

Mary walking in the cherry orchard. Now, she knew better, because there had been no miracle. No one had been saved—none had been spared. In a sense, Pétain's betrayal had sanctioned the killing of her husband and had left her childless.

Tuesdays and Thursdays, at 5:00 A.M., the sisters rose and dressed and ate a meagre breakfast of bread, hot milk and cheese. Sometimes in the hallway, leaving the house, they would encounter their neighbour from the floor above—the Catalan woman, Rosa Fuentes, whose job in the geriatric ward at the hospital required the same hours, five days a week, as the sisters' Tuesdays and Thursdays. Señora Fuentes would mutter and nod and go her way, but was always courteous and pleasant. Her gaze was sometimes haunted by an ageless innocence, an appearance, almost, of sanctity that transformed her. She might have been an icon in the transept, pale as stone, with carved, wide eyes. *Look*, she would say as they stepped out into the bright white morning air—*look how beautiful it is.*

3

The tiled and plastered house at number 22 rue d'Eté was the very house where the sisters had been born—five of them, over time. The two dead sisters were never mentioned, and in photographs where the five of them had appeared together, their figures had been scissored away.

On the third floor, where the ceilings sloped and there were dormer windows under the tiled roof, J-P Rousseau lived with his

Alsatian, Daisy. *It is good to have a dog in the house,* said Maryse, *in case of emergencies.*

And even better to have a man, said Thérèse.

In case of emergencies, said Babette.

The second floor of the house had once been rented to the Olivier family, whose children had been born and grew to maturity there. Only last autumn, the son and daughter had gone off to study at Aix and the parents had moved to a smaller apartment. The second floor remained vacant until the arrival in March, on a rainy day, of Rosa Fuentes and her daughter, Cristabel.

They were delivered in a cab.

Daisy was barking from the top landing. Thérèse told them not to worry. There was a gate and the dog could not get out.

Cristabel, who had not spoken, seemed to be alarmed by the barking. She stood beside her mother, almost as a child might have done, waiting to be told what to do. She must be in her early fifties, Maryse had concluded—judging from Señora Fuentes's age—and yet there was little to suggest her adult status. In repose, Cristabel's expression reflected a state not so much of permanent mourning—though she was solemn enough—as one of permanent longing. Something was missing, lost, unachieved—it could not be told—but the face had a curious beauty to it. Childlike, without being simple-minded—ethereal, without being vacant.

"You have come from Marseilles, so I understand," Maryse said, hoping to mitigate the tension engendered by Daisy's barking.

"She doesn't speak," said Rosa.

"Dear me, I'm sorry." And then: "but she hears. The dog ..."

"Yes, yes. She hears. But she does not speak."

"I see. Would you care for some coffee? Some wine, perhaps?"

"Thank you, no. We are tired. Good day."

That had been the extent of it. The Fuentes women took up residence and, aside from their footsteps overhead, the sisters were barely aware of their existence.

4

The first of the deaths was announced by J-P Rousseau, who worked in the town's mortuary as an assistant embalmer.

This day—it was late in June, on the day before Midsummer's Eve—he was on his way upstairs, with Daisy barking her welcome from above, when he paused with his hand on the newel post. He addressed himself to the parlour, where he was certain the sisters were sitting with their pastis.

"You recall Elena Moselle?"

There was a brief silence.

Someone whispered something and Maryse appeared in the doorway, wiping her lips with a handkerchief.

"Elena Moselle? That never married?"

"The same."

"Who did not return from the war for a dozen years and was rumoured to be dead?"

"The same."

"What of her?"

"The rumours are now true."

Thérèse and Babette crowded into the doorway, pushing Maryse into the hall.

Daisy went on barking and whining.

"Tell her to be quiet."

"Be quiet!"

Silence.

"What happened?" This was Thérèse.

"She was old," said Babette. "Almost eighty."

J-P Rousseau said nothing—enjoying the suspense.

"She was in the geriatric ward. I know that much," said Maryse. "Mindless, is what I heard. Not a shred of memory. Poor old lady."

"Well?" said Thérèse.

Rousseau fingered his hat.

"She was found in her bed with all her tubes and monitors removed—the IV hanging down and the oxygen tent pulled back."

Maryse blinked.

"What are you saying?" she said.

"He's saying that she committed suicide." This was Babette. She had read about such things in the papers—heard about them on TV. "It's common enough with the old. A person gets sick of lying on her death bed. Why not get on with it? I would."

"Is this true?" Maryse asked.

"So we're told," said Rousseau, irritated with Babette for having guessed the end of his story.

"Well, well, well," said Maryse. "Elena Moselle. Such a healthy girl she was. I remember her at school—a proper athlete. Wanted to be in the Olympics of '36—but much too young. And said it was her ambition to win the gold in 1940. Then the war, of course ..."

She narrowed her eyes. "She could outrun a horse, so it was said ..."

Thérèse snorted. "No one can outrun horses. What a joke."

"It wasn't a joke. There were people who swore they saw it."

"Anyway, she's dead."

"Yes. Poor Elena Moselle. Well."

"There you are, then," said Rousseau.

The sisters faded back towards the parlour, and J-P Rousseau went up the stairs to Daisy.

Half an hour later, Rosa Fuentes came through the front door. She declined the invitation from the parlour. "Thank you, no," she said. "There was a rather nasty death today and I'm tired."

"We knew her," said Thérèse.

"Did you. Well, then—I extend my sympathies."

"Were you there?"

"I'm afraid I was," said Rosa. She started up the stairs. "It was me that found her." And then, turning back: "don't tell Cristabel. Such things are hard for her to bear."

"Very well. Good night."

"Good night."

After Rosa had gone, Thérèse said: "I wouldn't have that woman's job, no matter what they paid me."

"I would," said Babette. "Sometimes the dying leave their money to their nurse."

"She's not a nurse. She's just a nurse-assistant."

"So?" said Babette. "I'd find a way."

5

Babette did not attend the funeral. Thérèse went reluctantly. She had but the dimmest image of Elena Moselle. Perhaps because of her age, it was not the enthusiastic memory that Maryse had dredged. What Thérèse remembered of Elena Moselle's athletic prowess was not her running but her bullying. The young were not safe in Moselle's presence. You were asked to scrub her back— you were asked to fetch her books. Still, she had been a local hero-ine. Everyone had marvelled at her strength. And her endurance. Moselle's name was synonymous with spirit—resolution—pride. Then, with the war, she had disappeared.

So it was said.

"There is more than one way to disappear," Babette told Thérèse. "But I was only a child. Perhaps my memory is faulty."

"What does that mean?" said Maryse.

"Nothing," said Babette. "I was young—and small. I knew nothing."

This was her constant theme. She felt herself to be in exile, in her tiny bones and half-blind state—an oddity to the rest of the human race, which was tall and robust and perfect. A world of Elena Moselles.

Maryse wore black; Thérèse, blue. During the mass, Maryse gave all the responses; Thérèse, none. Instead, she watched the flowers and listened to the music.

Judex ergo cum sedebit,
Quid quid latet apparebit:
Nil inultum remavebit ...

When the Judge shall take his seat,
All hidden things shall be made clear,
And nothing left unavenged ...

And nothing left unavenged, Thérèse thought. *Well—I could begin with all those books I carried ...*

When they got home, Maryse went on through to the parlour. Taking the cap from the pastis and pouring them each a thimbleful, she gazed at herself in the mirror.

Finally, Thérèse said: "have you nothing more to say about this death?"

"Nothing," said Maryse. "Why should I?"

"No good reason. I was just wondering."

Thérèse turned away and picked up a magazine. *Paris Match.*

Babette came down the stairs.

"I had the loveliest nap," she said. "I turned on the radio and fell asleep to Mendelssohn."

Maryse grunted. She seemed a great way off and alone.

Thérèse said: "there's a picture here of Marlene Dietrich's grave." She held up her magazine. "Did you know that all it says on the stone is *Marlene*?"

"Yes," said Maryse. "Another bitch."

"*Another?*" said Babette.

"Just an expression," said Maryse. "Like *another day.*"

6

J-P Rousseau, ever the gentleman, went to Rosa Fuentes and asked her permission to approach Cristabel.

"I'm gone all day, and Daisy gets so lonely. Also, she needs her exercise. In the past, the Olivier children used to walk her."

"Who are the Olivier children?"

"The Oliviers lived on this floor before you came."

"Ah, yes. I see," said Rosa. "You want Cristabel to walk your dog."

"Just so. If you would permit it."

"Why can't one of the Vergerines do it?"

"Well—they don't like Daisy, I'm afraid. Not in the park. They like her well enough in the house, but ... in the park ..."

"She attracts male dogs?"

"Just so."

"Of course." This was said smiling. And then: "you could have her spayed."

"She has been spayed. It makes no difference."

"A female is a female."

"Yes. Just so."

Rosa Fuentes looked from the window. There were the spires of the cathedral. There were all the roofs and chimneys turned in its direction. There was the sky—its birds and its clouds. There was the wind.

"I have never felt safe here," she said.

Rousseau was mystified.

"You've only been here since March," he said.

Rosa smiled. "Never can be since yesterday, monsieur." The smile faded. "Do you feel safe in this town?"

"But, of course. I was born here."

"I was born in Barcelona. You've heard of it?"

Rousseau blushed. "Yes," he said. "Everyone has heard of Barcelona."

"Everyone has heard of it, perhaps, but few remember its history."

"I don't think I understand."

"When I was a girl, in the 1930s, Barcelona was a living hell. Bombs fell on my childhood. They killed my parents."

"The Civil War?"

"The Civil War. Which France did not protest."

Rousseau was silent. He sat down. After which he said: "may I sit?"

"Of course"

They were in Rosa's parlour. Cristabel was in her bedroom, lying down. Evening.

Rousseau finally spoke. "Perhaps we did not protest—but in the war ..."

"In the war, you allied yourselves with the Germans."

"I did not do this."

"No. But your country did."

"All that is over. Please. It is 1996."

"True. I am not complaining, Monsieur Rousseau. Merely stating the facts. You want my daughter to walk your dog in the park. Can you guarantee her safety?"

"I don't quite understand ..."

"CAN YOU GUARANTEE HER SAFETY?"

Rousseau half stood up and sat back down.

Then he said: "the dog will be with her."

Rosa was satisfied. "Yes," she said. "I'm sure she will be delighted."

Rousseau stood again.

"Will you pay her?" said Rosa.

He had not intended to, but: "yes," he said. "Whatever you think is reasonable."

"Thank you. I will tell you in the morning."

"In the morning, then."

"Yes."

"Good evening."

"Yes. Good evening."

7

The next death occurred two days later. Louise Ferland—another enigma. This time, no one knew her.

"What was she doing in our geriatric ward if no one knew her?" Maryse asked.

There was no good answer.

J-P Rousseau, who had brought the news yet again, did say the woman had looked familiar. "My mother had friends whose name was Ferland and something of this woman rang a bell—but I was just a child. It was not the face so much as the expression ..."

Maryse could not help herself. She said: "the expression? When you saw her, she was dead, I presume. You remember a dead expression?"

Rousseau smiled. And shrugged. "A constant look of surprise. That's what I recall. But, still ..."

"Ferland is a relatively common name."

"Yes. But not in Villeverger."

"So you think she was a stranger."

"Possibly."

"Does it matter?"

"Well, it's just ... I wonder what she was doing here."

The question could not be answered.

8

Four days later, when the third death occurred, le docteur Leclerc called in the coroner from Toulouse. Leclerc was in charge of the geriatric ward and had become concerned when, on examining the corpse, he had discovered bruises on the forearms and shoulders.

This time, the woman's name was Marie Aubusson. Like Elena Moselle and Louise Ferland, she had been in the ward for almost one year and, like them, was senile. But unlike Moselle and Ferland, she had otherwise been healthy. Her death was sudden and quite unexpected.

The coroner was not able to come at once and was further delayed by the distance he had to travel. Toulouse was almost an hour away to the southeast and, it being a Friday, there was heavy traffic. When he finally arrived, he was frustrated and tired. "If I did not have to cover the entire district," he said—and threw his hands in the air. His name was Capron.

Leclerc took him down to the morgue in the basement and showed him Marie Aubusson's corpse.

"She looks as if she has been mistreated. Did she ever require restraints? Was she violent?"

"Not in the least. She was gentle as a child."

"Well, well, then. Let me take a look."

Half an hour later, he called Leclerc down and told him that Marie Aubusson had been murdered. Smothered. The bruise marks must have been made during the struggle.

"We must tell the police. It is my duty."

"Yes. And mine. But—oh, dear God! Our reputations. The hospital's. *Mine*. The head nurse's. *All* of them."

"You will survive it. Only one person did this—and once that person has been discovered, all will be well."

"But the newspapers ..."

"It is wisest not to suppress it. Someone will tell. It would look very bad."

"Of course."

"You make the call. I will speak to the Prefect. Then you can take me to dinner." Capron was smiling. "I am tired," he said. "We will eat and drink and tell each other stories. The rest is up to the police."

"Of course."

They returned to Leclerc's office and he placed the call. It was 5:35. By 6:00, the Prefect himself was on the premises.

9

J-P Rousseau said: "so—it has happened again."

"What?"

"Another death."

"Who was it this time?" Thérèse asked.

"Marie Aubusson."

"Marie Aubusson? God in heaven," said Maryse. "I remember her. Very well. I remember her *very* well. She sat behind me in high school. A devout Catholic. A very moral girl. She ..."

"Yes?"

"She ..."

"What, Madame Maryse? She *what*?"

"Nothing. I forget. She was ... serious. Overly so. I think she had few friends. She and Elena ..."

"Elena?"

"Moselle. Elena Moselle. They were ..."

"Yes?"

"People used to say that Marie Aubusson was Elena Moselle's pet. Followed her everywhere. Did her every bidding. It wasn't healthy. She might have been a slave."

"Just so."

Rousseau went upstairs and came back down.

"Where is Daisy?" he said. He was standing in the parlour doorway. All three sisters were present.

"Cristabel must be walking her."

"So late?"

"I heard her go out hours ago," said Babette.

Rousseau bit his lip. "My dog," he said. "If something has happened to my dog ..."

"What could have happened?" said Babette. "Nothing. She was on her lead. She could hardly run away."

"An accident," said Rousseau. "She could have been run over."

"Now, now. She'll come back."

"I'm going to go and look for her." He started towards the front door.

"No need," said Thérèse, who was watching from the window. "Here they come, now. And Rosa is with them. All is well."

The front door opened. Daisy came through first and then Cristabel.

Rousseau took a step forward and struck her.

Everyone froze.

"I was *frantic*!" he said. "How dare you! How *dare* you!" He struck her again.

"Monsieur Rousseau!" This was Rosa.

Rousseau snatched Daisy's lead from Cristabel's wrist. "She had no business staying away so long."

"She came to meet me at the hospital. I was delayed."

"SHE HAD NO BUSINESS!"

Maryse stepped forward and put her hand on Rousseau's arm. Cristabel was sitting on the stairs with her head bowed.

Rousseau said: "I can't have hurt her very much. Look at her. Not a sound."

"She has no voice," said Rosa. "And I demand an apology. How can you have struck a child?"

"She's a fifty-year-old woman!"

"She is a child." Rosa went to the stairs and lifted Cristabel to her feet. Then she turned to Rousseau and said: "apologize."

"She was away too long. The walk is only supposed to last an hour."

"Apologize."

He said nothing. Daisy was lying at his feet.

Maryse said: "M'sieur Rousseau. Please. Apologize and have done with it. Then it is over."

He thought about it—made a wry face—and then said: "I'm sorry."

"She can't hear you."

"I'M SORRY."

"Thank you."

Rosa pulled Cristabel aside and J-P Rousseau, with his dog, went up the stairs and slammed his door.

"Well, my goodness. What a display," said Maryse. "I hope he didn't really hurt her."

"Of course he hurt her."

"Yes. I suppose so."

"Come, my loved one, we will go now." Rosa turned Cristabel towards the stairs.

"We hear there has been another death," said Maryse.

"Yes. Madame Aubusson." Rosa paused. "There is going to be an investigation." She started up again.

"An investigation? Whatever for?" This was Thérèse.

"The coroner came from Toulouse. He says she was murdered."

"Marie Aubusson *murdered*?"

"Murdered. Yes." Rosa went on climbing. "It is none of our business. Good night."

10

On the Monday, permission was granted to exhume the corpse of Elena Moselle. Also the corpse of Louise Ferland. By this time, the press from Toulouse, the press and television from Marseilles and also from Montpelier had begun to arrive. Once the news broke that Moselle and Ferland had also been murdered, they came down from Bordeaux, Lyon and Paris. By week's end, Villeverger was the centre of the world.

One week after Marie Aubusson's death, Rosa Fuentes came into the sisters' parlour and said: "I have something to say."

J-P Rousseau was walking Daisy in the park. Clearly, Rosa had waited for his departure before she made her appearance. Cristabel was upstairs, watching from the window. She had not come down since Rousseau had struck her.

"Please," said Maryse. "Sit. You look tired. Surely you will accept some pastis."

"I will, this time, with pleasure. Thank you."

Waiting for Maryse's return from the dining-room, Rosa sat at the edge of her chair, one hand fisted in the other, while Thérèse and Babette settled back to hear what she had to say.

"What a beautiful evening it is," said Babette.

"Yes."

"Of all the summers in recent years, this is the best."

"Yes."

"Whole weeks of sunshine."

"Yes."

"And the thrush, whose nest is in the plane tree, has launched her young. They flew the coop today. I saw them."

"Yes."

"Such a lovely moment, when they fly."

"Yes. Yes, indeed."

Maryse returned with a silver tray bearing pastis for all, the bottle only newly begun. When she had passed the glasses, she set the tray on its table and sat down.

"Well," she said. "Here's to all of us. And may we thrive."

They drank.

Then she said: "and so?"

Rosa said: "yes. And so ..."

11

This is what Rosa Fuentes told the Vergerine sisters:

You know that I am Spanish. Catalan, from Barcelona. My parents died in 1939. February. I was there. And my sisters. I won't bore you. This is an old story—well known. For one week—every day, all day—the bombs fell. When the planes came, we hid beneath the stairs.

Six of us, one of us a baby. I was sixteen.

On the fourth day our house was hit. Both my parents—Dora, the baby—Marguerita—Alicia—all were killed. Only myself and Trina survived. For three hours, my mother's body lay on top of me, pressing Dora into my hands. The gift of a dead child.

Once we were rescued, there was nowhere for us to go. We looked for relatives, but all were either dead or taking part in the defence. A week later—maybe two, I don't remember—the city fell.

Trina was fourteen. I knew about rape. She did not. I knew we must leave Barcelona. It was a madhouse, with killings in the streets, everyone starving and the Rebels drunken and uncaring. A great many others—some with their possessions—were determined to make their way to France. And so, we joined them. Walking.

At first, we went up into Andorra—but they would not allow us to stay. A few refugees were still determined to reach France and I thought it was best for us to go on with them. Of course, this meant the mountains. We were freezing—sleeping in barns and out-houses, begging or stealing food. The journey took us fourteen days.

"On foot!" said Maryse. "And barely more than children. What an ordeal."

"Yes. It was."

"But at least you got here," said Thérèse. "At least you got to France."

There was a small silence.

Then Babette said: "yes—and we all know what's going to happen next."

"I don't," said Thérèse.

"You have the memory of a cow," said Babette. And then, to Rosa: "tell."

In France, we were interned.

"You see! I knew that."

"Be quiet, Babette."

Maryse had got out her sewing box and was tatting lace. She was creating a set of place-mats for the granddaughter of a friend. "Pay no attention," she said. "My sister is a know-it-all. Go on."

We were called political refugees. I knew we were foreigners, but my only politics—and Trina's—were the politics of fear. All we had wanted was not to be raped and not to die. Still, we were interned.

There were a number of us. A very great number. Hundreds. Men, women and children. This was in March. The war—the Civil War—would end in April and we all thought: when the war is over, we will be freed. We were wrong. France, and England, too, were the first to recognize General Franco as the legitimate head of state. We were then considered doubly political enemies—the enemies both of France and Spain.

_____

España, Rosa had said. Until then, she had spoken entirely in French. Now, not Espagne, but *España.*

"España. I never went home."

Babette said: "Cristabel is not a Spanish name. It is German."

No one spoke. And then:

> *Until 1942, we were only Spaniards in the camp. And then, towards the end of that year, General Pétain capitulated. M. Laval was given the power to rule by decree. The Germans came. You will, of course, remember this.*

Again, no one spoke.

> *One day, a convoy of trucks arrived, bringing a whole new population to our camp. Jews.*
>
> *I do not like Jews. In Spain, they have caused many problems. Over time, endless problems. The largest problem with Jews, of course, is that they are not Catholics. Be that as it may, they were our fellow prisoners. More and more of them arrived. The fences multiplied. The territory of the camp enlarged. Trees were cut down. We lived with stumps. And Jews. And Germans.*
>
> *This became another reason I do not like Jews. It was only because of the Jews that we got the Germans. Otherwise, only the French had been in charge of us. Now, all these thick, blond men and their thick, ugly*

*language. And their farness from home. And their need
for women.*

*Women. We were women. Young. Myself and Trina.
Others—maybe twenty of us. Thirty. One could not keep
track. You French at least had fed us. We were not starved.
Not yet. And we were—well, as I have said, we were
young. Supple. Pliant. Pretty.*

Thérèse gave a cough.

"Excuse me," she said.

*We were taken aside. Housed aside. When the time of star-
vation came, we went on eating. We had water. Showers.
Mirrors. A person could see herself. And we were given
uniforms. White. Like nurses. Wrap-arounds. You see?
Like this. No buttons, just a belt of cloth. And nothing
underneath. We had no underclothes. Nothing. Not even
underpants. Shoes, we had. Sandals. And our smocks. We
were allowed to keep our hair. And to brush it.*

*They would take us in the evenings. Trucks came and
moved us into another part of the compound. There was a
long, dim room. The men drank German beer. We were
given nothing. In a while, they would cross the room, pull
at our clothing and explore us with their hands. When they
were satisfied, we were taken into cubicles. A bed. A sink.
A spill of light through a transom. Rape.*

*I will not dwell on these events. I cannot. Let me tell you
only this. Trina, my sister, was made ill with syphilis. Once*

it was known that she was ill, they took her away to what they called The Infirmary. *A wall. A stone wall. In a yard somewhere.* The Infirmary.

"Why are you telling us this?" said Thérèse, all at once. "It is so unpleasant. Meaningless."

"Be quiet," said Maryse, not looking up from her work.

Babette rose and poured them all a second glass of pastis. Sitting down, she said: "we have dead sisters, too."

Maryse gave her a look.

Unperturbed, Babette finished: "and just like you, we never speak of them."

Time passed. It passed, though one barely knew it. The truckloads of Jews kept arriving—endless Jews and endless Germans. Endless, all of it. In 1944—I think—something happened. Changed. Two things. One—and then the other.

Empty trucks began to arrive.

Empty.

And went away filled.

With Jews.

Only Jews. No Spaniards.

And then, in the corps of women to which I belonged, there began to be Jewish girls. Twelve-year-olds. Fourteen. Children, who gave up their bodies to save their lives. Pretty girls. Dark haired, like us. Beautiful. To my amazement, one of these looked like Trina. Somewhat like Trina. Enough like Trina for me to befriend her. And ...

And she was ... in time, she was impregnated.

Of course, there was no protection. Ever. The men wore nothing. We were given nothing. Some women died, attempting to abort their babies. Others went to The Infirmary. *But my friend—whose name was Sophie Gephard—she did not want to abort her child. She wanted her child. She believed in life.*

More and more Jews were taken from us. Hundreds. Hundreds. Thousands. The camp began to seem a wasteland. Everyone was evil-tempered. Everyone, that is, in charge of us. Paris fell. The Allies landed in the south. The Germans began to flee. To leave us.

"I remember that," said Babette. "I remember them leaving—very well. Such a relief it was. They had stolen our food!"

And ours. This was when we all began to starve. In the camps, with no Germans, the French took back the duties they had given up when the Germans arrived. Not given up entirely, of course, but they had become supernumeraries— extras in a horror film. Do this. Do that. Stand here. Stand there. Kill that woman. Kill that man. *Et cetera.*

Thérèse gasped. "We never did that," she said. "We never killed those people."

Then she said: "you. We never killed you. Never."

Rosa said: "all of this happened in France, Madame Thérèse. All of this happened in France."

There was a silence. Short.

Maryse put aside her work and said to Rosa Fuentes: "come to the end. Explain."

> To the end, *you say.* Explain, *you say. It is all too simple.*
> *Our camp was liberated in 1944. The summer of 1944.*
> *In the panic that was engendered by the advance of the*
> *Allies from the south, many of us were killed. Almost as if*
> *... It was almost as if our keepers were afraid there would*
> *be no more opportunity to shame us—no more chances to*
> *humiliate and maim us. Also, if we lived, we would not be*
> *silent. They had been seen—and we would say so.*
> *Most of those in charge of us were men. But there were*
> *also women.*

Maryse adjusted her glasses, sipped at her pastis and began to fold her tatting into squares.

> *Some of these women ... Of course, one never wants to*
> *admit it, but women are just as capable as men of despica-*
> *ble acts—of inhumanity and cruelty. Of course they are. Of*
> *course they are. Of course we are.*

Thérèse put her hand over her mouth. Babette turned away. Maryse wavered and then continued her folding.

> *Not that I was one of them. Yet. I was a prisoner—not a*
> *guard. A whore—not a nurse. In those last days, before the*

liberation, women were lined up and shot down. The ill were poisoned. Troublemakers, certain to point fingers and name names if they survived, were hanged. I ... I was silent. I saw nothing—heard nothing. Knew nothing.

The arrival of Sophie Gephard's child was imminent. Such cruel timing. In a day—in two days—the Allies would arrive and free us. But the child would not wait.

We hid. My friend and I. We kept on moving—stopping only in the barracks where the culling had already taken place. We even lay amongst the dead ...

The birth took place at dawn. It was barely light at all. I cut the umbilical cord with a piece of stone. I wrapped the child in my prostitute's smock. Three women came to the door. They were drunk. Sophie said: go. Take the child and go. *She was too weak to move. Half starved—ill— and having given birth ...*

I ...

The three women came forward.

They were in uniform.

Drunk.

One of them had a revolver.

I heard a baby crying, *she said.*

I ...

Where is the baby?

There was barely any light. And many shadows. The birds had just begun to sing. I remember that so well. Bird-song. Finches. Blackbirds. A thrush.

My friend said: over here.

She spoke aloud.

Over here, *she said. There is no baby. It was only me.*

The three women found her.

I was watching. From my corner. My hand was over the baby's mouth. I was so afraid she would cry—but also afraid she would suffocate.

My friend began to wail.

They were kicking her.

She cried and cried and cried.

They forced her to her knees.

They made her crawl before them to the door. And through the door. And down onto the earth.

Babette could be heard breathing.

Thérèse put her face in her hands.

Then I heard the shots.

And laughter.

And then ... they went away.

Maryse finished placing her folded squares into her work box, closed it and set it aside.

"Cristabel?" she said.

"Yes. It was Sophie's middle name. Her parents had brought her out of Germany into France in 1937. Not that it did them any good."

"And the three women?"

Rosa said nothing.

Babette said: "Elena Moselle. Louise Ferland. Marie Aubusson."

Rosa Fuentes looked at her hands.

"How did you know they were here?" said Maryse—barely audible.

"Where else would they be? It is where they were born."

No one spoke.

Then Rosa stood up.

"Please," she said. "Come with me."

She led them into the hall and up the stairs. In her parlour, Cristabel sat by the window, gazing out at the darkening sky.

Rosa urged her to stand—and beckoned to the others.

"Look down there," she said. "What do you see?"

"I see the town," said Thérèse.

"The town, yes. The old town. But out there, farther off—where all the lights are coming on. You see? The walls—the fields—and the cherry orchards?"

"Yes."

"You know as well as I do what was there before."

"It was not us," said Thérèse. "We did not do this."

"Villeverger. Yes? The town. Its cathedral. And its concentration camp."

Thérèse sat down. Almost as if pushed. Maryse rubbed the back of her sister's neck and kissed the top of her head. "Never mind," she said. "Never mind. It is over."

Thérèse wept.

Rosa said: "I couldn't let them just die. I couldn't allow that. I was incapable. Incapable, you see, of forgiveness. That is what I meant when I said that I was not one of them. Yet. But now, I am. I am."

Her voice faded.

When the gates were opened, I carried Cristabel out into the fields. It was so incongruous. Crazy. There were all the cherry trees—and we, out walking in their shade. The cherries were not yet ripe. Still, I put one in my mouth. Sour and hard, yet its juices were filled with the promise of sweetness. We sat down. I sat down beneath the cherry trees with Cristabel in my lap—and looking back towards the town, I saw the spires of your cathedral. There it was, beyond the cherry branches, rising above these houses—rising above these roofs—and looking down at the concentration camp, where—in all those years we were there—its shadow had never reached us.

After a moment, Maryse said: "what will you do now?"

"What I must," said Rosa. She looked at Cristabel. "What I must for me—and what I must for her." And then: "she is ... Please," she said. "One of us must survive."

Maryse looked away for a second and closed her eyes. When she opened them, she said: "of course. She will be welcome here."

"Thank you," said Rosa. "In the morning, I will be gone."

"It's getting dark," said Thérèse. "Shouldn't we ..."

"No," said Maryse. "Let us stay here for a while. Later, we will go downstairs. Then we will turn on the lights."

12

In their long grey smocks, black stockings and rag-bound hair, the Vergerine sisters were known to everyone. To watch them drift beneath the vaulted ceilings, caught in the early morning light—here one, there another—skating between the pillars in their wide-mopped shoes, was to see some ancient ritual dance performed by ghosts.

There above them, gazing down through the flickering votive lights below her, the Madonna of the Cherry Trees—holding the Christ Child—watches the sisters come and go. *When the gates were opened, I carried Cristabel out into the fields.*

Her expression is one of gentle amazement. She puts her hand out, thinking perhaps to collect a cherry for her Child's amusement—even, perhaps, for his blessing. *And I sat down beneath the cherry trees, with Cristabel in my lap ...*

The sisters do not look back. There is more to do. There is always more to be done.

Angels and archangels—Virgins and Baptists—jewelled Saints and flaming Martyrs—all with dusted toes and polished fingernails. *No one knows this dust like we do. No one ever will. We will be here till we are part of it.*

The stones are as old as Charlemagne.

About the Author

TIMOTHY FINDLEY is one of Canada's best-loved and most-respected writers. He recently published his first novella, *You Went Away*, to widespread critical acclaim and bestseller status; his most recent novel, *The Piano Man's Daughter*, was a #1 national best-seller. His novels have garnered many prestigious awards: *Headhunter* received the 1994 City of Toronto Book Award, *The Wars* won a Governor General's Award for Fiction, and *The Telling of Lies* was the winner of the Edgar Award. His other novels, *The Last of the Crazy People*, *The Butterfly Plague*, *Famous Last Words*, and *Not Wanted on the Voyage*, as well as two collections of short fiction, *Dinner Along the Amazon* and *Stones*, have been tremendously popular with both readers and critics.

Findley is also noted for his dramatic works and non-fiction. *Can You See Me Yet?* was his first play to be staged, and *The Stillborn Lover* won a Chalmers Award. His 1991 bestseller, *Inside Memory: Pages from a Writer's Workbook*, won the Canadian Authors Association Literary Award for Non-Fiction.

In 1996, France honoured him with its highest award for artistic achievement, making him a Knight of the Order of Arts and Letters.

Timothy Findley divides his time between his Ontario home and the south of France.

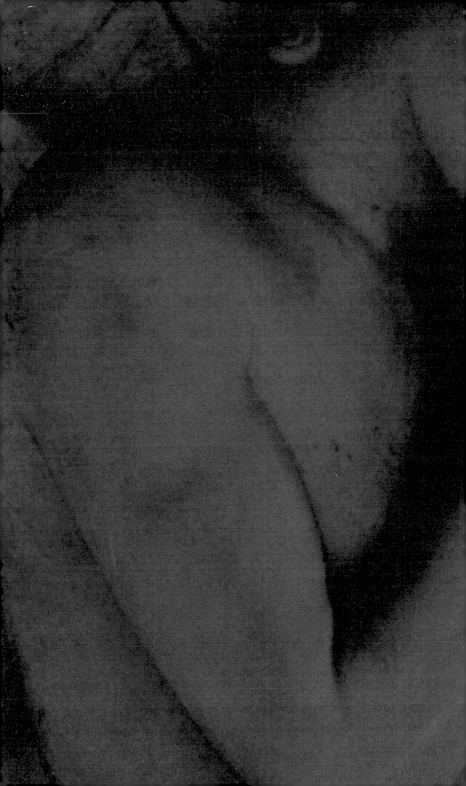